"I *have* no enthusiasm for this wedding."

Reece continued, his voice deep and unemotional, "And I have no intention of pretending I have."

"Then why are you spending so much money and making such a fuss?" Miriam asked.

"She is my sister. She is certainly more than old enough to make her own decisions and her own mistakes, but this…this is a mistake."

"But they might love each other!"

"Oh, spare me," he interrupted mockingly.

"I think you're being very narrow-minded. It's a well-known fact that opposites attract!"

Dear Reader,

Help us celebrate life, love and happy-ever-afters with our great new series.

Everybody loves a party and birthday parties best of all, so join some of your favorite authors and celebrate in style with seven fantastic new romances. One for every day of the week, in fact, and each featuring a truly wonderful woman whose story fits the lines of the old rhyme "Monday's child is…"

> Monday's child is fair of face,
> Tuesday's child is full of grace,
> Wednesday's child is full of woe,
> Thursday's child has far to go,
> Friday's child is loving and giving,
> Saturday's child works hard for its living,
> And a child that's born on a Sunday,
> Is bonny and blithe and good and gay.
>
> (Anon.)

Does the day on which you're born affect your character? Some people think so—if you want to find out more, read our exciting new series. Available wherever Harlequin books are sold.

May	#3407 *The Marriage Business*	Jessica Steele
June	#3412 *Private Dancer*	Eva Rutland
July	#3417 *Coming Home*	Patricia Wilson
August	#3422 *Desperately Seeking Annie*	Patricia Knoll
September	#3424 *A Simple Texas Wedding*	Ruth Jean Dale
October	#3429 *Working Girl*	Jessica Hart
November	#3434 *Dream Wedding*	Helen Brooks

Happy reading,

The Editors, Harlequin Romance

Dream
Wedding
Helen Brooks

Harlequin Books

TORONTO • NEW YORK • LONDON
AMSTERDAM • PARIS • SYDNEY • HAMBURG
STOCKHOLM • ATHENS • TOKYO • MILAN
MADRID • WARSAW • BUDAPEST • AUCKLAND

ISBN 0-373-03434-2

DREAM WEDDING

First North American Publication 1996.

This edition published by arrangement with Harlequin Books S.A.

CHAPTER ONE

'YOU aren't Bennett and Bennett? Tell me you aren't Bennett and Bennett.' The hard grey gaze was uncompromising as it swept over their faces, and Miriam swallowed deep in her throat before forcing a smile to her lips.

'The very same.' She gestured to her brother. 'Mitch Bennett, and I'm Miriam. How do you do?' As she held out her hand the tall dark figure in front of her turned abruptly, stepping back into the sumptuous hall with a cursory flick of his head.

'You'd better come in.' The tone was rude and aggressive, and for a moment they stood in bewilderment on the top step before following Reece Vance into the gorgeous, lavishly decorated surroundings.

'Mr Vance, I think—'

'Look, there's been some sort of a mistake.' Again he turned and fixed them with that icy glare. 'I was told I was going to meet the joint partners of a successful and thriving catering firm who could get me out of the mess I'm in with the minimum of fuss.' He eyed them angrily. 'Not a pair of teenagers who clearly—'

'My brother and I took over our father's catering firm on his death five years ago, Mr Vance, as I'm sure Mr Craven explained,' Miriam cut in quickly, desperately holding onto both her temper and her aplomb by the skin of her teeth. 'I'm aware we don't look our age, but that's hereditary, I'm afraid. However, we've had plenty of experience—'

'How old are you?' He almost ground his teeth at them. 'Both of you?'

'My brother is twenty-six and I'm twenty-five—'

5

'For crying out loud!' It was meant to be insulting, and as Miriam felt her face flame she remembered what Frank had told her.

'The man's under a lot of pressure, Miriam—his sister's wedding only two weeks away and the catering firm he'd employed under investigation by the police for fraud. He might be a little...touchy, but nothing you can't handle.'

'Excuse me,' Mitch said at her side, his tone almost as aggressive as Reece Vance's. 'It might have escaped your notice, Mr Vance, but no one dishes out any favours these days. It's dog eat dog. When my sister and I took over the business it wasn't doing too well.' The understatement of the year, Miriam reflected silently as she remembered the mound of debts and unpaid bills. 'And now we employ five other people besides ourselves—'

'Very creditable, I'm sure.' His tone was scathing. 'But this particular job would entail a staff of at least twenty on the day, not to mention all the preparatory work.'

'Of course it would.' Miriam smiled at him sunnily as she reflected that he was easily the most obnoxious, unpleasant, *detestable* individual she had ever met in her whole life. 'And my brother was just about to add that we have part-time employees prepared to work at very short notice.' Why have you done this to us, Frank? she asked silently as the grey eyes held her own violet ones in a vice. We might need work, but no one needs it this bad!

'And you think you can cope with this contract?' he asked icily.

'I've no idea, Mr Vance.' Her own smile died now and she stared at him straight-faced, her eyes disdainful. 'You haven't even begun to tell us what it entails, have you? Catering we can supply, but mind-reading comes extra.' Steady, Miriam, steady, she warned herself quickly as the grey eyes chilled further. This job could establish Bennett and Bennett for good if you pull it off; don't blow it on a temper tantrum.

'I would have thought Frank would have explained,' he said after a long moment of taut silence.

'He merely phoned us with a minute to spare as he boarded a plane for the States and gave us a time and your address.' Miriam tried another smile but it would have had more effect on a block of stone. 'He said you'd had some difficulty with the present caterers,' she added tactfully.

'You could say that.' He glared at her as if it were all her fault. 'Well, now you're both here you might as well come in the study for a moment and I'll explain what the job entails.'

His tone said, quite succinctly, that such a procedure was a waste of time, and as they followed him into a huge room just to the right of the stairs, which seemed to stretch forever upwards, she had the mad urge to kick him hard up his dignified and very regal backside.

'Now.' He sat down behind a large and expensive desk in beautifully polished walnut and gestured towards two easy chairs placed strategically in front of it. 'Do sit down.' He spoke as if he was bestowing an honour of the utmost proportions, and just for a moment Miriam's irrepressible humour asserted itself. What a stuffed shirt! What an overwhelmingly pompous stuffed shirt. He made her feel as though she wanted to do something outrageous to get through the hard outer skin that clothed this man like a barrier: take her clothes off and dance on his desk naked, maybe?

Her mouth curved slightly at the thought until she met the silver-grey eyes again, her gaze taking in the hard, high cheekbones and aquiline nose that at the moment was flared with something approaching distaste. No, perhaps not. On reflection, the thought of appearing anything but fully dressed in front of this man sent a little shiver snaking right down to her toes.

'Now—' the splintered gaze took in Mitch too '—I don't know how much Frank has told you, but let me fill you in on the details. My sister is getting married at the beginning of December—the second to be exact—and she is marrying an Australian with a host of relatives who are coming over *en masse* for the nuptials. Something, quite frankly, that I am not particularly looking forward to. With me so far?' They nodded silently; the tone was biting.

'The actual wedding breakfast for the two immediate families, which at the last count numbered just over one hundred and fifty, is no problem; that has been arranged separately at an excellent hotel.' He mentioned a name that made Miriam's eyes widen. She knew the place; one needed to take out a second mortgage to eat there, and this man had arranged a wedding breakfast for half of Australia on its premises? Rothschilds, eat your hearts out, she thought faintly as she tried desperately to concentrate on the precise, cold voice.

'However, Barbara, my sister, wanted to continue the rest of the celebrations in the family home—a buffet through the afternoon and evening, with dancing in the big hall and a firework display at night.'

The big hall? Miriam tried desperately to look unimpressed.

'We have over three hundred family and friends descending on this house, expecting food and drink in vast quantities, and at this time I have no idea how I'm going to accommodate them.' He eyed them grimly. 'The directors of the catering firm I had employed are at the moment in police custody, so I don't expect any help from them.'

With anyone else it would have been an attempt to lighten the conversation, but Miriam saw that he was speaking with no shred of amusement in either his face or voice, just a cold iron-hardness that was beginning to deflate even her natural optimism.

'I would expect a large selection of seafood and English dishes, another section devoted to Chinese and Indian cuisine, with at least nine hot dishes in each besides the attendant cold foodstuffs, and, of course, the appropriate choice of desserts. The whole lot would be cleared by six o'clock and cheese and biscuits, fresh fruit and strawberries and champagne served at precisely nine o'clock, when the firework display has finished.'

He looked at them both sitting in front of him, their bodies completely motionless, and as the cool, ironic gaze lingered on her face for an instant Miriam shut her half-open mouth with a little snap.

'You think you can handle all this? Before you reply, a word of warning.' The arctic gaze chilled further. 'The present catering firm will rue the day they let me down; prison will suddenly become an oasis in the desert I intend to make of their lives.'

He wasn't joking, Miriam thought faintly; he really wasn't joking.

'I pay for, and expect, the best—both in quality of service and the speed and efficiency with which my smallest wish is carried out. If you took this contract on and I was satisfied, you would find me most generous, both with your remuneration and the references that would be your due. If you failed me...' The icy grey gaze washed over their attentive faces and Miriam had to stop herself gulping like a schoolgirl.

'So?' He smiled grimly and rose from behind the desk. 'I presume you would like some time to think about your answer.' He didn't expect them to take it. As Miriam looked up into the patronisingly superior expression that the hard features had settled in she found herself speaking before she could stop herself.

'I would have thought time was of the essence, Mr Vance.'

'It is.' Just for a moment she saw a flash of surprise in the silver-grey eyes.

'Then I think, certainly from our side, we can let you know our answer immediately.' She felt rather than saw Mitch stiffen by her side, but something outside herself was driving her on and she was powerless to stop her next words, which she heard with a shred of horror. 'We would be pleased to take the contract if it is offered and we can assure you that all your requirements would be met most satisfactorily.'

'I see.' The silver gaze narrowed. 'And do I take it you are in agreement with your sister, Mr Bennett?'

Mitch's voice was slightly strangled but he backed her to the hilt. 'Of course.' He rose as he spoke and Miriam was conscious that Reece Vance dwarfed her brother's six-foot frame by a good few inches. 'We are a partnership.'

Black eyebrows rose a fraction, but beyond that Reece Vance didn't comment.

'We'll leave you our particulars, Mr Vance, and some brochures you may find of interest—'

'Why?' He cut into her polite farewell speech abruptly. 'If you are taking the job you will surely need to inspect the premises?'

'Taking...?' He had called her bluff. She hadn't expected him to offer them the job in a thousand years; it was right outside their league and he knew it. She *knew* he knew it.

The dark face was inscrutable, his manner relaxed, but she knew instinctively that he had responded to the challenge that she had been mesmerised into throwing down because he was a man who couldn't resist such a situation. He hadn't liked her response to him. She bit on her lower lip hard. And now he wanted his pound of flesh; he wanted her to admit that she had spoken foolishly. And she had.

'Come and have a look at the kitchens.' He was already walking out of the room and she found herself trotting after him with Mitch at her side, her brother's face stunned with the sort of blank vacancy that she was sure must be written all over hers.

How could she have been so impulsive, so foolish? How could she? She barely noticed the magnificent surroundings that they were passing through as her thoughts raced frantically.

When she and Mitch had taken over their father's tottering catering business on his sudden and totally unexpected death five years before, they had been met with a host of problems—not least their possible immediate bankruptcy. Their father had been no businessman; how the firm had survived as long as it had in his hands no one knew, and for two greenhorns fresh out of college, aged twenty and twenty-one respectively, to attempt to resuscitate the failing concern had seemed ludicrous to everyone but themselves.

But they had seen the blood, sweat and tears that had gone into their father's dream of a family business and both of them had felt that they couldn't just sit back and see the vultures move in. And so they had worked. And worked. And worked. And it had only been in the last year that they had begun to see the reward.

Their name was getting established and their reputation assured; they were, at long last, out of the red, and for the first time in several long years the nightmares that accompanied each pay-day for their five faithful employees were a thing of the past. And now she had possibly thrown it all away. She felt her heart thud painfully. She would have to eat humble pie, tell him they couldn't possibly—

'This is the big hall I spoke of.' She came out of her panic to find that they had just entered what appeared to be a massive ballroom, its ceiling lofty and the high, curved walls gracious. 'It's an extension to the original house. My mother loved to entertain when she was alive and so my father had this place built on.

'It has its own kitchens, which are separate from the original one which serves the rest of the house; they are situated at the back of the hall down a corridor where there is also a small flat. You would be welcome to use that if you felt it necessary to stay on the premises to oversee everything.'

Oversee it? She glanced up, and up, at the dark man by her side—the tall, powerfully built body seemed to dwarf her slim, five-foot-eight-inch frame—and noticed that the hard, tanned face was really very attractive. The thought didn't help and she dragged her mind back to the task at hand. Oversee it? She and Mitch would be working every hour of the night and day if they took this thing on, and then some.

'Come along.' Like a pair of obedient puppies they followed at his heels again as he crossed the beautiful wide expanse of exquisite parquet flooring which seemed endless before opening a carved oak door at the far end and waving them through. 'Here are the kitchens.' A few yards down the wide, white-walled corridor was another door which he opened with a flourish. 'I think you will find everything you need.'

As Miriam preceded him into the room, followed by Mitch, she felt a dart of excitement pierce the panic for the first time since her disastrous impulsiveness. The kitchens went on and on, gleaming bright and beautifully furnished with every available modern appliance known to man amid space and more space. To work in such surroundings would be heaven.

She glanced at Mitch and could read the same thoughts on her brother's face. Everything could be done on site—everything—and that alone would make the whole job so much easier.

She wandered down the length of the vast room, turning to find that it went on still more in an L shape, the far end having a magnificent view over immaculately tended gardens that stretched into the distance before disappearing into what appeared to be a large wood.

'It's just . . . just—'

'Functional?' He'd interrupted her dazed voice drily but as she glanced at him again she saw that the dark face was smiling, and the effect was riveting. Whether or not it was the shaft of white sunlight glancing in from the massive windows, she didn't know, but she hadn't

noticed before that his hair was so thick and black, or
that the lashes which curtained the silver-grey eyes were
so profuse. He was undeniably male, and the strong features and aquiline nose were too aggressive to be classi-
cally handsome, but he'd got something. He'd certainly
got something, she thought weakly. 'Come and see the
flat.'

They retraced their footsteps out into the corridor, and
directly opposite another door opened into a beautifully
sunny little flat complete with small lounge, bedroom,
shower room and a tiny but expertly fitted kitchen.

'There's only one bedroom, I'm afraid.' He glanced
at them with eyes narrowed against the bright winter
sunlight. 'But the sofa extends into a double bed, should
it prove necessary.'

'I—' She took a deep breath and swallowed before
trying again. 'What exactly are the financial—?'

'I would expect you to buy whatever you need; there
will be a blank cheque with regard to that side of things,'
he said coolly, gesturing for them to be seated on the
sofa as he perched on the side of a small writing desk.
'I won't be looking over your shoulder every two
minutes, but I would expect a receipt for everything pur-
chased, of course, and I want both food and drink to
be of the best quality. The champagne for the evening
supper is already taken care of, but the wines and spirits
along with everything else will be down to you. Your
own fee will be the same as I was offering the other firm.'

When he said the figure she almost asked him to repeat
it. It was a small fortune—*a small fortune*.

'And, of course, your employees' salaries and travelling expenses will be met by me separately through you.'

She was glad that she was sitting down.

'You can forget references or anything of that nature,'
he continued quietly. 'Frank is an old friend of mine—
as I understand he was of your father—and his word is
better than any written confirmation as far as I am concerned. So...' He stood up suddenly, his masculinity

seeming to fill the small room. 'Is it a deal or are you having second thoughts?'

'Mitch?' She wanted to take the job; against all rhyme and reason she wanted to take it, even knowing that they were going to be stretched to breaking point and beyond, but, as Mitch had pointed out a few minutes earlier, they were partners and she had had no right to accept it without consulting him first. 'What do you think?'

Mitch stood up slowly and walked across to Reece Vance with his hand outstretched. 'You have a deal, Mr Vance. If you are prepared to take a chance—'

'Oh, I'm not taking any chances.' The cold voice was derisive. 'There will be schedules to meet and it's of no concern to me whether you have any sleep in the next two weeks or not. What is of vital importance is that everything goes smoothly on the day, and to that end you will work every hour it takes to make my sister's day a happy one. And it *will* be happy.' As Miriam joined them she saw that the silver eyes were as hard as stone. 'Won't it, Miss Bennett?'

'Yes.' She raised her small chin as she spoke, her red hair flaming in the sunlight that filled the pretty room. 'It will.'

'Good.' His smile was totally without warmth. 'Then we understand each other. If you would care to accompany me back to the main house I'll iron out some of the formalities with you and we can sign whatever needs to be signed.' He ushered them out of the flat as he spoke and they were halfway across the vast hall before he spoke again. 'Unfortunately my housekeeper fell downstairs this morning and broke her ankle; she and the maid are at present at the hospital. However, I can offer you a cup of coffee—or perhaps something stronger—'

'The poor woman.' Miriam looked at him aghast.

'Yes.' He eyed her grimly. 'However, my sympathy is somewhat tempered by the fact that she was carrying far too much at the time—something I have warned her

about over and over again—and the accident has had
the effect of making a difficult situation well nigh impossible. A temporary housekeeper will be more trouble
than she's worth, especially now—' He broke off as he
made an exclamation of irritation. 'And for crying out
loud stop looking at me as though I've developed horns,
would you?'

'I'm sorry.' Miriam lowered her head quickly before
the urge to say more spilled over. She had never met
such a heartless brute in all her life. Was he for real?

'So what do you intend to do?' Mitch asked quietly
as they walked through into the main part of the house
again and towards the room that they had vacated a few
minutes earlier.

'There is little I *can* do,' he replied tersely. 'Obviously
Mrs Goode will have to do the best she can with limited
mobility, but muddling through is not an activity that
appeals to me, Mr Bennett. I can, and shall, employ
temporary staff while my guests are in residence, but it's
inconvenient—damn inconvenient.'

'Can't your sister help?' Miriam ventured tentatively
as he waved them to the two seats in front of the desk
again. 'I know it's a busy time for her but—'

'Exactly.' He eyed her frostily. 'And frankly, Miss
Bennett, once you have met Barbara you will understand why I have no intention of letting her loose on my
household; the results would be chaotic.'

He raked his hand through his hair in a gesture that
spoke of immense frustration. 'And it shouldn't be
necessary anyway. Everything was organised most
capably by my secretary three months ago, when Barbara
announced her engagement. I paid an inordinate amount
of money in order to secure the services of first-class
companies to prevent this very thing from happening.'

'Well, the best laid plans of mice and men . . .' Miriam
said philosophically. 'I'm sure it will all work out
in the end.'

'Then you are more confident than I, Miss Bennett,' he growled tightly, his scowl indicating his opinion of her optimism. 'Now, I can spare you a further five minutes so let's go over the bones of the thing.'

By the time they left, exactly five minutes later, Miriam knew that she loathed Reece Vance. He might be fabulously wealthy and live in the sort of mansion that she had only seen in glossy magazines; he might be more—much more, if she was being honest—than averagely attractive, with the sort of rough, he-man sex appeal that some women found irresistible, but to her he was—the pits.

She glanced at him now on the doorstep as he towered over them, his harsh, dark face and narrowed eyes infinitely cold. *Definitely* the pits. Rude, aggressive, unapproachable... The list was endless.

'I shall expect one of you here tomorrow at ten o'clock to make contact with Mrs Goode,' he said abruptly.

'That's no problem.' Miriam nodded quickly. 'I'll come; Mitch has an appointment.'

'Right.' The tone was terse. 'And you'll bring a rough outline of what you propose, along with time schedules and—'

'I'll bring all that's necessary.' He hadn't liked her interrupting him—she could see it in the silver-grey eyes that reflected the cold winter sky overhead—but now she smiled cheerfully as she held out a small, slim hand for him to shake. 'Goodbye, Mr Vance. We have an appointment shortly, so do excuse us rushing off.' It was a blatant lie but it was either that or giving in to any of a number of impulses that were running through her mind, all of which would have had dire consequences on the prospect of their employment.

'Goodbye, Miss Bennett.' As he took her hand in his she was suddenly conscious of the feel of his warm, hard flesh encompassing hers, and a little flicker of sensation shivered right down to her toes, bringing her soft violet eyes wide open with surprise. She wanted to snatch her hand away, to object somehow, but in the next instant she was free anyway as he turned his rapier-sharp gaze to Mitch.

She stood, more shaken than she cared to admit, and watched him as he said goodbye to her brother, noticing that there were flecks of silver in the jet-black hair that added to rather than detracted from the virile magnetism of the man.

He frightened her. The thought was there before she could control it and, once given life, shocked her. But it was true. There was something about him that had nothing to do with his outward appearance—a dark force, a fascination, compelling and cold and quite unfathomable, that she had never, ever come across in her life before.

'Till tomorrow.' He dismissed them with a cool nod but didn't step back inside the house as she had expected; instead he stood and watched them walk over to their little beaten-up jalopy, his eyes burning into the back of her head. She suddenly found that she didn't quite know how to walk, was vitally conscious of her body in a way she never had been before, and breathed a soft sigh of relief as she pulled open the door and sank down onto the moth-eaten seat.

'Well, what do you think?' Mitch turned to her as he slid into the car beside her with a slightly dazed grin, which faded as he noticed her pale face. 'What's the matter? You aren't having second thoughts about this now, are you?'

'Just start the engine and drive the car, Mitch.' She knew, without looking, that he was still there on the steps, the big, lean body relaxed and indolent as he watched them leave and the hard, superior face alert, silver eyes intent.

'All right, all right.' The car took several seconds to flare into life, as it always did, and by the time Mitch persuaded it into a semicircle and they passed the house

Reece Vance had gone. It was only at that point that she relaxed back in the seat.

'It's no good looking like that, Mim,' Mitch grumbled softly at her side as he negotiated a small patch of black ice in the middle of the long, winding drive that led from the grounds surrounding the house to the main road in the far distance. 'You were the one who jumped in with both feet. I thought you wanted to accept the job anyway. What—?'

'I do, I do.' The interior of the car was even colder than the icy weather outside, and she blew on her hands before wrapping them under each armpit. 'I'm just not looking forward to seeing any more of him, that's all.'

'Why?' Mitch turned the heater on and then quickly off again as a blast of arctic frost seared their faces. 'I'd better let it warm up a bit first.' He turned to her for a second, his face enquiring. 'Why don't you want to see him again?' he asked mildly. 'I thought he was OK, and the deal is one hell of a generous one if we can pull it off.'

'Of course we can pull it off,' she said firmly, her voice determined. 'It's the chance of a lifetime for a small firm like ours, and if we do a good job he might recommend us to a few of his friends. It's just...' Her voice trailed away as her brow wrinkled. 'He's so rude and abrupt—'

'The guy is in a bit of a spot, Mim,' Mitch said quietly, his tone so reasonable that she immediately felt guilty. 'First the caterers rocking the boat and now his house-keeper out of action. It'd make anyone...edgy.'

'Hmm.' Miriam eyed him carefully. 'Well, how about if I do the Baker job tomorrow and you come back here, then?'

'No way.' The response was instantaneous, followed by the sheepish smile that Mitch did so well. 'You know you're the one to deal with any difficult customers; you never let anyone get to you like I do.'

'There's always a first time.'

'You'll be fine.' Mitch patted her hand in a gesture that was meant to be comforting but was merely irritating. 'You probably won't see him again anyway. Moguls who generate that amount of power and money don't sit at home twiddling their thumbs, Mim; they're out making the city hum or whatever they do. Now, what we've got to do tonight is sort out a plan of action and go for it. If I deal with the jobs we've got on at present and leave you clear to concentrate on this until I'm needed does that suit you?'

'Does it matter if it suits me?' Miriam asked resignedly.

Mitch smiled cheerfully as he gave her a swift hug. 'That's my girl! How many part-timers can we call on, anyway?'

They discussed tactics and figures until they got back to the office attached to the small factory unit they rented, whereupon Mitch disappeared to organise the job for the next day, leaving her alone with her thoughts.

It was only after a good ten minutes that she found she was daydreaming about a host of possible situations she might find herself in, where she could put Reece Vance very firmly, and with great composure and coolness, in his place. Wherever his place was. She grimaced to herself helplessly. He didn't fit into any mould or slot that she could think of, that was sure. But, like Mitch had said, it was highly improbable that she'd see anything at all of him over the next few days—*of course* it was.

She gave herself a mental shake and applied herself to the task at hand, but it was harder than normal to concentrate. A cold pair of silver-grey eyes kept getting annoyingly in the way—so much so that at five o'clock, when the others left, she was still far from finished.

When the phone rang at just after six she picked it up automatically, her thoughts on the time schedule she was pencilling in, and then almost dropped it as that particular cold male voice barked the firm's name. 'Bennett and Bennett?'

'Yes.' Her voice was weak and she heard it with a strong burst of self-disgust. 'This is Miriam Bennett speaking,' she added more firmly. 'How can I help you?'

'This is Reece Vance; we met earlier.'

'Yes, Mr Vance?' He's going to cancel, she thought helplessly as a strange feeling coursed through her limbs. Would she be relieved? He'd obviously made enquiries and gone for one of the more up-market firms who were all window-dressing and caviare. She couldn't blame him, but—

'I'm afraid Mrs Goode is still in hospital,' he said grimly, 'which rather upsets the arrangements for tomorrow.'

'Oh, I'm sorry.' She desperately tried to appear businesslike but there was a definite tremble in her voice when she spoke again. 'She's more badly hurt than you thought?'

'The break is a complicated one.' Miriam would have hated to be in the poor housekeeper's shoes next time she saw her employer; even with several miles between them she could feel the angry vibes flowing down the phone. 'She'll be operated on tomorrow morning and hopefully be home within a few days. The thing is, as you so rightly mentioned this afternoon, time is of the essence.'

There was no sarcasm in the deep voice but she felt herself blushing as she remembered the emotion that had prompted her words.

'I wondered...' He hesitated for just a moment. 'I wondered if you could start to organise things without her. Jinny, the maid, will help all she can, but it will put even more pressure on you, I'm afraid. Mrs Goode has been with the family since Barbara and I were born and knows everything and everyone; I was banking on her to clear the way for you, so to speak.'

'It's no problem, Mr Vance.' The sudden relief she had felt told her that she *did* still want this job, very badly. 'A job of this nature is ninety-nine per cent preparation work, and you've provided both the resources and the finances for that to go smoothly. There won't be any problems we can't overcome.'

'You're very positive.' There was a note of approval in the hard voice for the first time and it was ridiculous how much it pleased her.

'So I'll still come to the house as arranged?'

'Yes, please. I'll be there myself and we can—'

'There's no need for that.' She had spoken quickly, far too quickly, and the blank silence at the other end of the phone told her that the rapier-sharp mind knew it. 'I mean...' She paused as she searched the air frantically for a way to say exactly what she *didn't* mean, the truth being insulting. 'I know you must be a very busy man, and this sort of thing is my job, after all. There won't be anything I can't handle—'

'Ten prompt, Miss Bennett.' As the phone went down she stared at the receiver in her hand with her heart thudding and hot rage taking the place of embarrassment. He'd hung up on her! How dared he? She bit her lip painfully. Not even a courteous farewell or a thank-you! They were certainly going to earn every penny of this undertaking.

She lounged back in the padded seat and shut her eyes, taking a few deep, calming breaths. She wasn't going to let him get to her. The resolution suddenly crystallised in her mind.

This was ridiculous. Here she was expending all this hot rage and energy on someone she would never meet again once the next two or three weeks were over, and it wasn't like her—it wasn't like her at all. She was the sunny-natured one of the partnership, always looking for a silver lining when Mitch presented them with dark storm clouds, and, what was more, usually finding it. No, for some reason which she couldn't quite fathom she had allowed Reece Vance to get under her skin from the first moment she had met him, and it had to stop.

Right now. She nodded to herself determinedly and suddenly felt miles better.

She'd do the job he was paying her so handsomely to take care of and she'd do it well. She'd pull the proverbial rabbit out of the hat, work twenty-four hours a day, eat humble pie till it came out of her ears, whatever it took. She nodded again. It wouldn't be too difficult. After all, two weeks was a mere hiccup in her lifespan and Reece Vance was only a man like any other, even if he did think the world revolved around his particular orbit.

CHAPTER TWO

'YOU'RE late.' She had flung herself out of the taxi and hurtled up the steps to the huge, studded front door, her briefcase clutched protectively across her chest and her cheeks flushed, but just as she'd raised her hand to the bell the door had opened to reveal Reece Vance's scowling dark countenance in the aperture.

She stared at him now as her mind went momentarily blank, and then pulled herself together sharply. 'I know.' She took a deep breath. 'I'm sorry, Mr Vance, but the car wouldn't start and I had to get a taxi at the last minute.'

'By "car" do you mean the vehicle you travelled in yesterday?' he asked grimly as he stepped aside and ushered her in with a jerk of his head. 'I'm not surprised it wouldn't start; the very fact that the thing has four wheels amazed me.'

'Really.' All the good resolutions of the night before went flying out the window as she struggled to remain civil. 'Well, I can assure you it's normally quite reliable. How is Mrs Goode this morning?' she added stiffly.

'Petrified of the anaesthetic,' he answered surprisingly as he led the way, not into the room of yesterday, but into a huge, luxuriously furnished drawing room where a massive log fire, set back under the ornately carved mantelpiece, dominated the room with its warmth and colour.

He turned and gestured to a large, winged leather chair pulled up close to the flames. 'Do sit down. I've managed to organise coffee and cake, if that's all right? Jinny is staying with Mrs Goode at the hospital for the time being as the poor woman is quite beside herself at the thought

23

of an operation.' A certain note in the deep-timbred voice told her that he found such an attitude unfathomable.

'Lots of people are nervous of hospitals.' She smiled politely but he looked at her blankly.

'How illogical.' He was dressed more casually than the day before, when he had worn an elegant, light-weight suit. Now the tall, powerful body was clothed in loose grey cotton trousers and an open-necked shirt, and the effect on her senses was...disturbing. The broad, muscled shoulders and strapping chest were impressive, but it was the whole compelling aura of the man that she found unsettling—his raw, untempered masculinity too vigorous, too dominating for comfort.

She held onto her smile through sheer will-power and glanced round her surroundings with what she hoped was cool aplomb. 'What a beautiful room.' She settled herself in the chair and prayed for composure. 'You are fortunate to live in such lovely surroundings, Mr Vance.'

'Could we drop the formality a little?' he asked abruptly as he continued to look down at her from his considerable height. 'We're probably going to be seeing a great deal of each other over the next two weeks, and "Mr Vance" is already beginning to grate.'

'Oh.' She stared at him, taken aback.

'And as you are Frank's godchild I think I can trust you not to take advantage of any familiarity.' She thought that she caught a throb of amusement in the deep voice but his face was perfectly straight as he looked at her, his silver eyes narrowed on her upturned face.

'Yes...' She was flustered and it showed. 'Well, I have some costings here, Mr Vance—'

'Reece,' he interposed smoothly.

'Reece.' She knew that her pale, creamy skin was burning a bright red but there was nothing she could do about it. Unfortunately this annoying tendency to blush went hand in hand with the dark red hair her parents had blessed her with. 'I think...um... What I mean is—'

'I'll fetch the coffee and then we can talk.' He had left the room before she could react, and as the door closed behind him she sank against the soft leather back of the chair with a hard sigh.

This was ridiculous! She wasn't a young, skittish schoolgirl who couldn't string a sentence together, she was a mature businesswoman well able to cope with whatever came across her path. She put a hand to her chest, where her heart was thudding as though she'd done the four-minute mile. She had to pull herself together, she really did.

She opened her briefcase quickly and spread out some of the papers on the coffee-table by her side, her eyes skimming the neat columns of figures and detailed schedule. She had to convince him that Bennett and Bennett knew what they were about, and the first step was stringing a coherent sentence together!

She smoothed her smart grey skirt over her knees and pushed a stray tendril of hair behind her ear. She wouldn't be overawed by this man, she just wouldn't; there were plenty of people as rich and influential as he was after all.

But it wasn't exactly his wealth that she found so intimidating, was it?

She shut her mind to the little voice that probed annoyingly. Well, whatever it was, the job was all important, and if she wanted to get any sort of a reference from Reece Vance at the end of it she'd better remember exactly that.

He returned almost immediately with a tray holding a pot of fragrant coffee, two stylish mugs and a very large fruit-cake, along with milk, cream and sugar. 'How do you like your coffee?' He bent down at the other end of the coffee-table as he spoke, placing the tray on its polished surface, and she felt her nerves jump at his closeness.

'White, with cream and sugar.' The black eyebrows rose a little and she laughed apologetically. 'I know; not

exactly healthy, but I like it that way. I'm a great be-
liever in the old adage that a little of what you fancy
does you good.'

'Oh, so am I,' he said gravely, with the merest inflexion in his voice which nevertheless sent the colour
surging back into her face. What was it with him? she
asked herself irritably. She could normally socialise with
anyone—laugh, even flirt a little—but somehow Reece
Vance had her nerves as taut as piano-wire.

Once settled with her coffee and an enormous slab of
fruit-cake, she cleared her throat determinedly. 'I've got
the main points dealt with in this lot—' she waved a
hand at the papers by the tray '—but I was wondering
about some of the details. Do you want us to do the
flowers or has that been arranged separately? And what
about—?'

'Drink your coffee first.' His voice was very deep—
at least three or four decibels lower than the average male
voice—and extremely attractive with a husky edge... She
caught at her wayward thoughts, horrified at the way
her mind was going. 'Then we'll go through the items
one by one so you'll know exactly what I require of you.
From that point on you are on your own unless there
are any technicalities that crop up in future days.' She
nodded without speaking and took a big gulp of the hot
liquid, hoping that it would soothe her jangled nerves.

'Barbara will be coming down this weekend on a flying
visit,' he said after a moment or two of silence. 'I'd like
you to meet her and show her the relevant details, if
that's possible?'

'Of course.' She nodded at once. 'She doesn't live here,
then?'

'No. My sister has her own flat in the City.' He smiled
coolly. 'Her independence is everything to her—or was.'

'Oh.' She didn't know quite how to respond to that.
'And your parents...?'

'They have been dead a number of years.' It was said
without any apparent emotion and her face straightened

at the cold tone. She glanced up to find the silver-grey eyes tight on her face. 'My parents were...social animals,' he said calmly. 'My sister and I were sent away to boarding-schools as soon as we could toddle, and family life as you probably know it just didn't exist for us. Consequently I have no real feeling of loss at my parents' death and no wish to become a hypocrite and pretend one.'

'I wasn't criticising—'

'Yes, you were.' He eyed her grimly. 'Your face is very open, Miriam. I can call you Miriam?' She nodded helplessly, wanting to lower her eyes away from that hypnotic gaze but quite unable to do so. 'Very open and very innocent. Quite an unusual combination in this fast, modern age. Do you live by yourself?'

The sudden change of direction threw her, and she gazed at him silently for a moment before nodding slowly. 'Yes.' She didn't quite like the personal tone that the conversation was taking but couldn't have explained even to herself the reason for her unease. 'Mitch still lives with my mother at home, though. She likes having him there to worry over and he enjoys having his washing done and his meals ready on time, but I found that after a couple of years away fending for myself at college I needed my own space.'

'No flatmate?' he asked expressionlessly, his eyes wandering over the gleaming red of her hair that glowed in the light from the fire.

'Not exactly.' The unease intensified but the dark face portrayed nothing more than polite interest. 'It's not really a flat anyway, just a small bedsit, but it's in a nice house and we have fun.'

'We?'

'The others who live in the house,' she said awkwardly. 'There are five bedsits and we all share the bathroom and kitchen so it pays to get on.'

'It would do.' He seemed as though he was going to say more, but after a long moment of silence settled back in his chair abruptly.

She finished the coffee and struggled through the enormous piece of cake, feeling more uncomfortable than she had ever felt in her life—and it was all down to him, she thought silently. He made her feel gauche and young and stupid, and yet, today at least, he had been quite civil. But it was just his whole attitude. She studied him through her eyelashes as she finished the last of the cake. He was so cold and severe, so without warmth, and yet...

'Right.' As she set down her plate on the coffee-table the piercing silver gaze switched to her face. 'Let's get on with it.'

And get on with it they did. He ran his eyes down several columns of figures, his lips moving slightly as though he was checking the totals, but Miriam couldn't believe that he could work so fast until she pointed out an error, his voice terse.

He was calculating the figures more swiftly in his head than she had done on the calculator, she thought weakly as he continued to skim over her neat lists, making the odd alteration here and there and one or two suggestions that were spot on. They had finished within ten minutes, although she felt as if she had left her brains somewhere back on the first couple of pages.

'Excellent.' He gathered up the heap of papers and handed them across to her. 'When do you intend to begin work?'

'Monday?' she asked carefully. 'I thought I'd take advantage of the four freezers in the kitchens if that's all right; it seems silly not to. And although I understand the fresh flowers will need to be put in place on the actual morning I wondered if the silk displays could be done during the previous week? With such a short time span ahead it would help—'

'Fine, fine.' He waved an impatient hand, clearly irritated by the minor details, but without the housekeeper being available it was essential that she got such factors clear at the outset, she thought determinedly. 'Anything else?' he asked abruptly.

'Would it be possible for me to familiarise myself with the kitchens now?' she asked quietly. 'I shall be bringing two assistants on Monday and I'd prefer to know where everything is.'

'Certainly.' He glanced at his watch as he spoke, his expression preoccupied, and as he strode from the room she trotted after him in much the same manner as the day before.

When they reached the big hall and began to cross it she felt a surge of rebellion as she followed the straight, hard figure in front of her—an illogical defiance against his cool command and authority.

She stopped abruptly, lifting her head to the magnificent, sculptured ceiling as she spoke. 'This hall seems tailormade for something as romantic as a wedding,' she said loudly, her eyes flickering to the broad body as it turned, and then back up to the ceiling again. 'Your sister is very lucky,' she continued a little breathlessly. 'She's going to have the sort of wedding every female dreams of.'

He eyed her for a long, sombre moment before replying, so her eyes were forced to drop to his face. The light streaming in from the tall, narrow windows either side of the building illuminated the thick black hair with a soft haze, and the hard grey eyes were narrowed against its brilliance as he took the few steps to her side. 'Satin and lace and orange blossoms?' he drawled cynically, his voice dark and sardonic. 'Something along those lines?'

'Sounds good to me.' She smiled, determined not to be intimidated.

'And you think such a beginning is important?' he asked mockingly.

'Important?' She stared up into his face, her nerves registering the sheer sensuality of the man at such close range. 'Not exactly important, I guess, but nice for those who can afford it.' The mocking curve to his mouth deepened and she stepped back a pace, her face straightening. 'What's the matter? Don't you agree?'

'Whether I agree or not is irrelevant,' he said slowly as his gaze wandered to her indignant mouth and then back to the angry violet eyes. 'The bare facts of the matter are that my sister is marrying a man she became engaged to after four weeks and has known for four months because she is suddenly, and quite irrationally, frightened of reaching middle age without the prospect of having children.'

His voice was deep and unemotional. 'She is not without charm and looks, has an extremely high IQ, which she uses to devastating effect in her job as a top lawyer, and yet, for some unfathomable reason, she has embarked on what can only be a major disaster for herself and the man in question. I'm sorry, Miriam, but I have no enthusiasm for this wedding and no intention of pretending I have.'

'Oh.' His words had stunned her, and with the silver-sharp eyes still holding hers her thought process was numbed considerably. She broke his gaze by sheer will-power, turning on her heel and pretending to glance round the beautiful empty hall as she struggled to get her thoughts in order. 'Then why are you spending so much money and making such a fuss?' she asked weakly.

'She is my sister.' There was an inflexion in the dark voice, the merest huskiness, that told her that he wasn't quite so detached about his sister as he would like her to believe.

'Are you sure it's true, what you've said?' she asked after a long moment had passed in absolute silence. 'I mean, how do you know—?'

'Barbara wouldn't acknowledge it but it is the truth.'

As she turned to face him again she saw that he appeared quite relaxed as he watched her, his arms folded over his chest and his muscled legs slightly apart. Relaxed and very formidable.

'I suppose it is inevitable, being twins, but I understand the way she thinks even when I don't agree with it. At thirty-five she has decided that the next stage in her life is a husband and children and made a cold-blooded decision to that effect. Nevertheless, she is certainly more than old enough to make her own decisions and her own mistakes, but this... this is a mistake,' he finished grimly.

'But they might love each other—!'

'Oh, spare me,' he interrupted mockingly, a hard edge to his voice that belied the relaxed composure. 'Her ardent swain is a full ten years younger than Barbara, a sports fanatic who could double for any Mr Universe, and was, I understand, thrown out of school as soon as it was legally possible. The epitome of all brawn and no brain. Now, does that sound like a love match to you?'

She stared at him uncertainly.

'This ridiculous farce might have stood a chance if he was from a similar background, nearer her age, if they had a few shared interests at least—'

'I think you're being very narrow-minded.'

'*What?*'

'I think you're being very narrow-minded,' she repeated bravely as she watched the black brows draw together and the grey eyes take on a decidedly arctic chill. 'It's a well-known fact that opposites attract and they might be desperately in love, for all you know. Just because she wants children it doesn't mean she doesn't love her fiancé, does it? And age doesn't matter, not at all.'

'Really?' His lips curled derisively. 'And the fact that she is an extremely wealthy woman in her own right and he is nothing more than a beach-bum doesn't matter, either, I suppose?'

'Not if they really love each other.' She held the hard, cynical gaze without flinching as he laughed mockingly.

'Good grief, girl, are you real?' His tone was scathing, and as hot colour flooded her cheeks she would have given the world to walk up to him and hit him very hard across his coolly patronising face. 'Rose-coloured glasses might be understandable in children, but I would have thought you were way past such nonsense. From what I've told you any fool would be able to see—'

'I am not a fool, Mr Vance, even if it satisfies something in your male ego to treat me like one.' Goodbye, lovely, lovely job, she thought faintly as she spoke. Mitch would probably roast her alive but nothing, nothing in the world could have stopped her speaking her mind. 'Your sister clearly hasn't told you that any of what you suspect is true and it seems to me that you are judging her fiancé more on his humble status than anything else. You think he's after her money, is that it?' She stared at him angrily. 'Well, is it?'

'Partly.' He pivoted on his heel as he spoke. 'And now, Miss Bennett, would you like to continue doing the job you are going to be paid handsomely to do? *You* may allow yourself the indulgence of time-wasting but I do not.'

He had reached the end door before she could collect herself sufficiently to move, and then she scuttled after him in exactly the same manner which she had berated herself for earlier. He held open the door for her to pass, his face icy, and as she brushed past him, her shoulder touching the hard, masculine chest for the briefest moment, she felt the contact in every nerve of her body.

He stood in one corner of the huge kitchens while she opened cupboards and poked and prodded into odd corners, searching out this utensil and that without saying a word, but she was vitally conscious of his dark presence as he leant broodingly against one white wall, arms folded and eyes narrowed.

Well, he was the one who had started the conversation, she thought angrily as she closed the last of the cupboard doors and stood up to leave. What had he expected? That she'd just listen without offering an opinion of her own? Perhaps that was the sort of female he usually associated with. She glanced over at the big, tall body as she nodded brightly. 'All finished.' Yes, he was definitely the type of macho man who would expect his women to be of a certain mould—malleable and amiable.

'Where are you going now?' he asked abruptly. 'I've an appointment in the City this afternoon, so if you don't mind waiting for a few minutes while I change I can drop you off on my way.'

'There's no need,' she said quickly. 'I'm going back to the office but I can easily call a taxi. I don't want to put you to any trouble and—'

'Don't be ridiculous.' He moved across to the door and opened it, gesturing her through. 'You can wait in the drawing room; I won't be long.'

He wasn't. No more than five minutes or so. But in that time her stomach had knotted itself into a tight mass at the thought of the proposed journey. It was a good fifteen minutes to the office from here and what on earth was she going to talk to him about in all that time? And how did one make conversation with a block of stone anyway?

She heard his hand at the door just in time to compose her features into a bright smile as he walked into the room, but in the next instant her heart was thudding desperately. The dark hair was slicked harshly back, the big body clothed in a dark grey suit topped by a heavy black overcoat which sat on the massive shoulders with brooding severity, and overall he looked dangerously attractive and utterly, totally, overwhelmingly male.

She gulped deep in her throat as the silver-grey gaze passed expressionlessly over her face. 'Ready? You'll have to direct me once we are off the dual carriageway; I'm not familiar with the address.'

'It's really very kind of you.' She could feel that with very little effort on her part she would begin to babble like a demented parrot if she wasn't careful, and as she followed him out into the hall he waved a hand towards the front door. 'I'll just bring the car round; you can wait on the steps.'

'Right.'

When the car appeared—an imposing and very beautiful pale gold Bentley—she forced herself to walk carefully down the steps. He had left the car at her approach to open her door, and now waited while she slid inside before shutting her door and returning to the driver's seat. The old-fashioned courtesy was unexpected and, she suspected, totally natural, but it didn't help the flutters in her stomach which his nearness produced as a faint whiff of expensive aftershave teased fleetingly at her nostrils.

'Seat belt on, please.' She jumped at the sound of his voice and then realised that she had been sitting like an idiot instead of fastening her seat belt—something she normally did automatically.

'Sorry.' She tried a small smile but he was concentrating on moving away and didn't glance at her again.

His harsh profile was disturbingly magnetic. He must have the women absolutely flocking after him, she thought weakly as the powerful car scrunched down the drive towards the far gates. That austere coolness was incredibly fascinating when combined with the aura of unlimited wealth and broodingly cold good looks; it would make any woman want to get underneath the dark, tanned skin and find out just what made this man tick. She caught at her thoughts with a shred of horror. No, it wouldn't. Not her, anyway. She must be stark staring mad even to consider—

'From what Frank tells me your little business is surviving quite well despite the economic climate.' The deep, husky voice at her side cut into her thoughts abruptly.

'You've obviously worked very hard over the last few years.'

'And how,' she answered, with more feeling than grammar.

'What made you decide to take on what was obviously going to be an uphill struggle?' he asked quietly. 'And at such a young age?'

She shrugged slowly. 'A number of things, really, but the main one was that both Mitch and I felt Dad would have wanted it that way. He'd worked for years to try and get the business off the ground; it had always been his dream for the family to have their own company, and we felt we had to at least try.'

'I see.' He spared her a swift glance before his eyes returned to the road ahead. 'You obviously loved your father very much.'

'He was a lovely man,' she said quietly, her expression introspective now. 'I can't ever remember Mum and him having a cross word although I suppose they must have done—probably when we were in bed.' She smiled to herself. 'They were always so protective of us; Mitch and I have been very lucky.'

'Yes, you have.' There was something, the merest shadow in the flat voice that swung her eyes to the grim profile, but she could read nothing in the harsh features to indicate what he was thinking. 'And your mother?' he asked expressionlessly. 'Does she work in the firm too?'

'Mum?' Miriam smiled at the thought. 'No way. She helps out at the odd function now and again when we need her, and is always available in an emergency, but she is no businesswoman. The house is full of dogs and cats—five dogs and six cats at the last count, although that has varied through my childhood—but she is a real homebody and we wouldn't change a hair of her head.'

'I see.' The sombre voice was thoughtful. 'You obviously had an idyllic childhood, Miriam; that explains—' He stopped abruptly.

'Explains?' she asked curiously.

'Explains your rather sunny attitude to life,' he answered shortly.

She stared at him in surprise, not at all sure if the comment was a criticism or a compliment but rather suspecting the former. 'You'd rather me be miserable, then?' she asked carefully after a long moment of silence.

'Not at all.' He shot a swift glance at her face and she saw the hard mouth curve slightly. 'And it wasn't meant in a derogatory way. If that's how it sounded I apologise. I'm sure your optimistic approach must have been a great asset to the business.'

'Sometimes.' She eyed him out of the corner of her eye. 'And sometimes not.' His smile deepened and she felt a ridiculous sense of achievement that she had actually made him smile, along with a dangerous weakness in her knees as the sensual pull of the man intensified. The sooner she was out of this car the better, she thought helplessly. She didn't exactly like him but... But he certainly had something and it wasn't doing her pulse rate any good.

'Mitch usually blames it on the nursery rhyme,' she said quickly into the silence, which had suddenly become charged with something she couldn't quite fathom. Something that was making little trickles of electricity flicker down her spine.

'I'm sorry?'

'You know.' She was speaking too quickly, but suddenly the close confines of the car were painfully intimate. '"Monday's child is fair of face" and so on.'

'I'm afraid I don't.' He shifted slightly and she was hotly aware of the hard bulk of him as the long legs readjusted their position. 'Nursery rhymes didn't play a part in my childhood, I'm afraid. They were an indulgence my parents did not approve of so my education is sadly lacking in that area.'

'Oh.' She stared at him, nonplussed. 'Well, it goes something like this, I think:

Monday's child is fair of face,
Tuesday's child is full of grace,
Wednesday's child is full of woe,
Thursday's child has far to go,
Friday's child is loving and giving,
Saturday's child works hard for its living,
But the child that is born on a Sunday
Is bonny and blithe and good and gay.'

'And you are?'
'I was born on a Sunday.'
'Ah...'
The rest of the journey was completed in virtual silence. She tried to make conversation once or twice but Reece seemed to have other things on his mind and answered in monosyllables discouraging further dialogue. They got to the office without any mishap although she got her lefts and rights mixed up once—something she had never done before, and which grated on her overwrought nerves like barbed wire.

'This is your home from home?' He glanced at the neat little office as they drew into the tiny square of car park.

'Yes.' She glanced at him uncertainly as he kept the engine running. 'Do you want to have a look round? I think—'

'Some other time.' He opened his door as he spoke and had moved round the bonnet before she could protest, opening her door for her and offering her his hand as she slid out of the car into the cold frosty air. His flesh was warm and firm and the contact seemed to shoot right down to her toes as she stood up, dwarfed by his great height.

She raised her head to make a polite farewell at the same moment as his glance moved from the building to the left of him and down to her face, and as their eyes held and locked she felt a sudden thudding in her chest. 'Your hair is like fire against the background of this grey sky,' he said softly as he continued to hold her hand in his. 'Warm and alive and glowing with passion. Are you passionate, Miriam?'

'I...' She couldn't speak. The grey eyes, their darkness soft and warm, had lost their chill, and the metamorphosis was as frightening as it was unexpected. She had never thought a man's touch, the expression in his eyes could set her body trembling helplessly, but she was experiencing it right now, and mixed with the excitement was an overwhelming sense of his male power. He was devastatingly experienced, an accomplished man of the world, and she had never felt her naïvety in the sexual realm so strongly as at this minute.

She had had a couple of boyfriends at college, but things had never progressed into anything beyond warm, prolonged kisses and the odd time of somewhat furtive fumbling, because she had always called a halt before any undue intimacy had begun. And, since taking on joint responsibility for her father's firm, every minute of the day and night had been accounted for simply to enable them to keep their heads above water—a fact that had grated on Mitch more strongly than her.

'I don't know,' she managed at last, and then was desperately humiliated at what the hesitant words had revealed to the darkly intent face in front of her.

'You don't *know*?' His amazement was the last straw, and as she pulled her hand jerkily from his, her cheeks flushing a deep, hot scarlet, she took a step backwards instinctively.

'No, I don't know,' she said tightly, her chin tilting upwards as she surveyed him with angry violet eyes, her mouth defiant. 'What's that, a crime?'

'I...' She wasn't to know that it was the first time that Reece Vance had been lost for words for a long, long time. All she knew was that he had guessed that she was a virgin. At the age of twenty-five. 'No, of course it isn't a crime,' he said softly after a long, tense moment had passed. 'It's—'

'Not for the want of opportunity,' she cut in tightly, her stance aggressive. 'I just don't happen to be one of those women who think it's necessary to seal every date in bed. All right?'

'It's fine by me, Miriam.' She thought that she detected a glimmer of amusement in the careful voice and glanced at him sharply—that really *would* be the last straw—but the dark face was as straight as a die and his eyes were totally serious as they stared back into hers.

'Good.' She turned on her heel and stalked off to the office building, feeling an absolute idiot and hating him for it.

'I'll give you a call about the weekend,' he called after her, his voice so devoid of expression that it was an indictment in itself.

'What?' She swung round sharply.

'You were coming to the house to meet Barbara?' he reminded her urbanely. 'I would like her just to OK some of the details.'

'Fine, fine.' She took a deep breath and tried to speak as one should to an employer. 'No problem.'

'Goodbye, Miriam.' He was still standing just as she'd left him by the car, and now she couldn't quite fathom the look on his face. Was it regret, a dark ruefulness, disappointment? She caught herself sharply. Dammit, he'd got her imagining all sorts of things now. She just knew that Mitch should have handled this job; this man was way out of her league and she didn't like the way he made her feel—she didn't like it at all.

'Goodbye, Mr Vance.' The formality was deliberate, but beyond a slight raising of the dark eyebrows he made no comment, walking lazily round the magnificent car whose engine was still purring, and sliding into its interior with a brief wave of his hand.

'Damn, damn, damn...' As she watched him drive away she found that she was speaking through clenched teeth, her cheeks still burning with colour. She'd never been so embarrassed in all her life. She opened the office door and collapsed into her chair as she groaned out her humiliation. What a thing to say. She must have been mad, but somehow, standing so close to him like that, all lucid thought had left her head. She groaned again and put her hands up to her hot cheeks. What was he thinking? What *was* he thinking?

'It doesn't matter what he thinks,' she said out loud to the empty room. She wasn't ashamed of her virginity—she wasn't—so why should she care what a man like him thought about her? After the next two weeks she'd never see him again in her life so it didn't matter a jot, not a jot.

But the world in which he moved was populated with cool, sophisticated women who were the epitome of elegance and good taste. She shut her eyes tightly as her mind replayed their conversation over and over. He must think her so gauche, so without social repartee. She could have made a light, throw-away remark to defuse the situation, which had started with a compliment to herself, and the whole thing would have been taken care of in the nicest possible way. She opened her eyes and glared at the opposite wall.

Well, she hadn't done that, had she? And she wasn't sorry. Not a bit of it. She wouldn't play his sophisticated, cosmopolitan kind of games anyway—not that she'd get the chance again after this. The thought didn't help, and she found that she was grinding her teeth again.

'Oh, blow it...' She reached angrily for her briefcase, determined to start work, only to realise that she had left it, along with all the relevant papers, in the back of Reece's car, where he'd placed it after he'd helped her in.

'I don't believe this.' She sank back in the seat helplessly. She was destined to make a fool of herself in front of this man and it didn't bode well for the next two weeks. It didn't bode well at all.

CHAPTER THREE

'MISS BENNETT?' As her head jerked up from the papers on the desk Miriam saw two bull-necked, stocky men standing in the doorway to the office.

It had been half an hour since Reece had left, and after deciding that he couldn't have noticed her briefcase when he'd returned to the car she had decided to stop crying over spilt milk and get on with the mountain of paperwork she'd been putting off for days. She could attack the Vance job tomorrow, when she'd retrieved the briefcase. Mitch and the others were out at a special reception in the City so she had at least three hours to work in peace, apart from the odd interruption of the phone.

'Yes?' She smiled politely even as the hairs on the back of her neck rose in protest. There was something menacing about these two, although she couldn't have described exactly what.

'Miriam Bennett, co-partner with Mitch Bennett of Bennett and Bennett?' It could have been a comedy routine, but there was nothing funny about the looks on the two men's faces as they moved to stand in front of her, their stance aggressive.

'Yes.' She wasn't smiling now. 'What can I do for you?'

'It's not what you can do for us, sweetheart, more a little matter of what you can do for Mr Gregory. You do remember Mr Gregory, I presume?' The one who seemed to be spokesman smiled thinly, showing blackened teeth stained with nicotine.

Miriam tried to keep the distaste out of her voice as she replied carefully, standing up as she did so, 'If you mean Mr Gregory of Turner's Garage then yes, I do.

41

My brother and I bought the firm's vans there just over a year ago.'

'That's right, sweetheart.' He nodded to the other man with a leering grin. 'I told you she would be co-operative, didn't I, Fergus? Now then . . .' He turned to her again. 'I believe Mr Gregory wrote to you a few days ago explaining the position you're now in, but you've been a very naughty girl; you haven't replied to him, have you?'

'I understand our solicitor has.' Miriam looked straight into the broad face as she spoke, squaring her shoulders. Bully boys. She might have guessed.

When Mitch had bought the two vans from Turner's she had thought the hire-purchase conditions a little steep, but Mitch had insisted that the vans were ideal for what they wanted and in good condition so she had gone along with the deal despite her misgivings.

And then a letter had arrived a few days ago declaring that they were behind with their repayments and informing them that the vehicles would be repossessed within the week. She had immediately questioned Mitch, who had shamefacedly drawn out of his coat pocket a stack of envelopes that he had forgotten to post the month before, but when she had phoned Turner's to explain the mistake the secretary had been less than helpful, insisting that the machinery to repossess had been set in motion and that there was nothing they could do about it.

Her solicitor had been more forthright.

'Turner's?' He had stared aghast at their faces and then back at the letter. 'You didn't go to Turners, Mitch? That man Gregory has had more brushes with the Old Bill than I've had hot dinners, and only just operates within the law now. Let's have your agreement.'

He had run cursory eyes over the paper and nodded with a deep sigh. 'He can do it—legally, that is—but it's a stinking agreement with the odds stacked in his favour. Do you realise that you only have to be one week late, according to this, and they can repossess? And you have to repay the rest of what you owe?'

'You're joking.' Miriam had turned to Mitch slowly. 'Didn't you read it, Mitch?'

'I read a sample agreement he had in the office, but it wasn't like this one.' Mitch had raised tortured eyes to hers. 'And when I signed after the deal was agreed I just assumed everything was OK. I didn't check it.' He'd run a shaking hand over his face. 'So there's nothing we can do?'

'Certainly there is.' Their solicitor had brightened at Mitch's explanation. 'First thing, I'll send a letter explaining we're not happy with the repossession and why, and stating that if it goes to court you'll testify accordingly. Old Gregory might back down at that; he's trying to keep a low profile these days. If that doesn't work we'll think again.' He'd smiled comfortingly. 'He might decide you're two little fish who aren't worth the trouble you could cause and leave it at that.'

But he hadn't.

Miriam took a deep breath and spoke firmly. 'You know your boss pulled a fast one on my brother, don't you?'

'Nothing to do with us, sweetheart.' The man shrugged carelessly. 'We're here to pick up the vans.'

'You're not having them.' She glared at the pock-marked face furiously. 'My brother isn't here anyway.'

'All by yourself?' He turned to the other man again and smiled slowly. 'She's all by herself, Fergus; now ain't that a shame?'

The other man nodded, running his dark little eyes over Miriam's figure. 'For her, maybe.' His eyes narrowed on her breasts before moving slowly upwards. 'Yeh, for her.'

'You don't frighten me,' Miriam lied tightly. 'Your Mr Gregory is a crook—'

'Now I'd watch your mouth, sweetheart, 'cos that's slander,' the first man cut in abruptly. 'An' Mr Gregory only wants what's legal. Your brother signed and he was over twenty-one; the rest's history.'

'We'll take it to court,' Miriam said angrily. 'Our solicitor said—'

'You don't want to take no notice of them solicitors, sweetheart.' Now the mean face was really nasty. 'And Mr Gregory don't like no courts and such like. If you behave you'll be all right; we'll leave you alone. You talk about courts, though, and we'll have to show you how things really are in the big, bad world. It'd be a shame if this lot was torched one night, wouldn't it...?' He sighed loudly. 'Or if that nice brother of yours had a little accident that left him in a wheelchair? Funny old world out there, love; you never know what's going to happen next.'

'Get out of here.' She was shaking, and furious with herself that they could see it.

'We'll just leave a little something on account first, to show you that we mean business.' As the one called Fergus moved towards her, his intention plain, she backed towards the wall, glancing at the first man appealingly.

He shook his head at her, laughing as his partner reached her side. 'He's an animal, sweetheart; I'd play along with him if I was you. No point in spoiling that pretty face of yours.'

'What the hell is going on in here?'

As the man nearest her spun round Miriam thought that she was going to faint with relief. She flew across the room to Reece's side and as his arm went automatically round her waist she saw that his hard face was dark with rage.

'I hope for your sake that what I saw when I walked in here can be explained,' he said tightly as his piercing grey eyes cut into the faces of the two men who had drawn together in front of the desk. 'But it had better be good.'

'Says who?' Fergus laughed sneeringly.

'Says me.' Reece thrust his car keys into Miriam's hand without looking at her. 'Go and get into the car while I teach these two gorillas some manners.'

'No, Reece.' She caught hold of his arm, panic-stricken. 'There's two of them.'

'She's right, guv'nor.' The first man smiled ingratiatingly. 'No point in getting hurt over a little misunderstanding. My mate and I are just leaving.'

'Think again.' He moved Miriam behind him, still without taking his eyes off the two figures in front of him. 'Lock yourself in the car, Miriam.'

'I'm not leaving you in here with them,' she said shakily. 'They were sent to collect our vans, Reece; they're strong-arm types—'

'The hell they are.' His laugh was sinister and totally without humour, and it seemed to have the same effect on the men watching him so closely as it did on her. 'You think you can push my lady around? Well, think again.'

'Look, we don't want no trouble.' There was an element of fear in the coarse voices now, and the brutish faces were uncertain as they glanced first at Reece's big, powerful body and then at his dark face, in which the silver-grey of his eyes glittered with unholy fire. 'We're just doing our job, guv'nor, that's all.'

'Which is?'

As the whining voices explained their mission Reece's icy gaze didn't falter.

'Well, now, you can go back to your Mr Gregory and tell him the situation has been resolved to the satisfaction of all parties.' Reece reached into his inside pocket and the two men flinched as his hand withdrew. They clearly wouldn't have been surprised if he had been holding a 44 Magnum in his fist. He threw a card onto the floor. 'Pick it up.'

The two hit heads in their eagerness to obey and for the first time since they had come into the office Miriam felt a glimmer of amusement break through the horrific fear.

'The contract has been terminated as from this moment, and your Mr Gregory will receive the outstanding amount on the vans within twenty-four hours. Not the hire-purchase mark-up.' He fixed them with his icy gaze. 'The residue against the original purchase price. Any queries he can refer directly to me. And *only* to me—got it?'

'Right, guv'nor.' Their heads were bobbing like demented pigeons.

'And now I think an apology is in order.' He drew Miriam into the fold of his arm. 'And it had better seem like you mean it.'

By the time the two men left, positively slithering past Reece, their faces averted, Miriam had begun to feel as if she were caught up in some kind of gangster movie, with the chief hood as her protector. He said not a word as he watched the two leave in a flashy red American job, and didn't relax his hold on her waist until he drew her back into the office, when he leant against the wall, his eyes closed, and expelled a long, expressive sigh. 'And I only came back to give you your briefcase.'

She stared at him, dumb with the shock of it all, and then as he opened lazy silver-grey eyes saw that his face was alive with a wry kind of amusement. 'I thought we might be in a spot of trouble there for a minute—before I realised they were all wind and water, that is. Still, the bodyguard act impressed you, I hope.' He levered himself off the wall slowly. 'And how did you come to be mixed up with a crook like Gregory anyway?'

'You know him?' she managed faintly.

'I know the type,' he said cynically. 'I've met a few like those two in my time—hired hands, with no brains—'

'Oh, Reece.' As she burst into tears he moved quickly and enfolded her in his arms, his face straight now, and somehow the big, muscled body seemed like a haven of protection after what she'd just passed through. He stroked her hair silently, making soft, comforting sounds in his throat, but when her sobs developed a touch of hysteria he moved her away from him gently with a little shake before staring down quietly into the drowning violet eyes.

'Enough.' There was a note of tenderness in the deep voice that added to her misery, although she couldn't have explained why. 'You can rest assured those goons won't be back when their esteemed boss knows he might be taking on the Vance Corporation. He might be a mean little swindler, and something of a villain, but I doubt if he's got brain damage.'

'That man, he was going to—'

'Don't think about it.' Reece reached for her coat and picked up the office keys on the desk. 'I doubt if they would have followed through on anything physical; they were trying to frighten you.'

'They succeeded.' She smiled shakily. 'Thank you so much— '

'I'm taking you to lunch so lock up,' he said expressionlessly.

'But you can't— Your appointment—'

'There is no fun in being the boss if I can't cancel when I feel like it.' He was trying to aim for lightness, but as her lip quivered again he pulled her into his arms and spoke into her hair. 'You aren't staying here, Miriam, and for the time being at least I shall want assurance from that brother of yours that there are always a couple of people about. This is not a particularly salubrious district at the best of times.'

'You think they'll come back?' she asked weakly, her voice muffled against his hard chest.

'No, I don't think they'll come back,' he answered, with the sort of light, teasing approach one favoured with children. The tone hurt, and she pulled away slightly to look up into his face. He thought that she was an inane, pathetic, fatuous type of female, and nothing she had done or said in the last few hours indicated any differently. She sniffed determinedly and forced back the tears with resolute doggedness.

'I'm not going to let them drive me out of my own premises,' she said firmly. 'I'm not.'

'Very commendable, but for today at least you are having a break.' He glanced at his watch. 'It's too late for me to keep my appointment now anyway, so if I can just use your phone and talk to my secretary we'll go and eat. A couple of stiff drinks and you'll forget today ever happened.'

No, she wouldn't, she thought faintly as she watched him make the call, his large bulk seeming to fill the small room. If she lived to be a hundred she would never forget the overwhelming relief she had felt when she had heard his voice. And he had handled those men so well.

She let her eyes wander over the hard profile as he concentrated on his call, his voice terse and rapid. He made every other man she had ever met in her whole life fade into oblivion...

Her eyes opened wide as she realised what she had just thought and she closed her mind firmly. She was grateful to him—of course she was—and everyone knew that one felt some sort of attraction for their defender in such a situation, and as a white knight he sure had a head start. Although she doubted very much if his morals were up to the standards of those crusaders of long ago. She smiled to herself at the thought at the same moment as he turned from the phone.

'A smile?' The dark face expressed its approval and she was immensely thankful that he couldn't read her mind. 'Can I ask why?'

'I was just thinking of how you dealt with those two,' she said quickly, her cheeks flushing.

'You sure do bounce back, Miss Bennett.' There was something in his glance that brought the colour flaring more hotly to her face. 'Sunday's child again?'

She nodded in reply.

'Well, that little rhyme has a lot going for it from where I'm standing.' As he took her arm and ushered her out of the office she could feel his hand burning through her coat and wondered again at her body's immediate response to this man.

He was cold and hard—look at how he had been about his poor housekeeper's accident, not to mention his comments on his sister's proposed marriage, she told herself firmly—and she sensed that he could be capable of great ruthlessness; those hired thugs had known it too. And yet... For some reason every minute she was in his company this physical attraction was getting stronger. She'd never felt like this about a man before, hadn't even know it was possible outside romantic novels.

She glanced at him as they walked over to the car waiting regally in the tiny car park. She shouldn't be having lunch with him. No good could come of it. She was probably going to make a worse fool of herself than she had already and she didn't trust herself around him. He had a great deal of something that she couldn't define, but whatever it was it didn't bode well for her peace of mind.

He settled her in the car as he had before and then walked round to his side, taking off his overcoat and slinging it on the back seat before sliding in beside her. 'I hope you didn't mind my insinuating to those thugs that you were my girlfriend,' he said mildly as he turned the key in the ignition. 'It seemed a good idea at the time.'

'Of course not.' She didn't know how to reply and knew that her cheeks were burning again. 'I doubt if they believed you, though.'

'Why is that?' He turned to face her as the big car purred gently.

'Well, it's obvious, isn't it?' She smiled nervously, but there was no answering warmth in the hard face watching her so intently.

'I must be very obtuse, Miriam; humour me,' he said drily.

'Oh, come on, Reece.' He wasn't making this very easy but she was blowed if she was going to make a worse fool of herself than she had already, by playing Cinderella to his Prince Charming. Perhaps he had sensed that she was attracted to him and thought that she was hoping—

'Why wouldn't they have believed me?' he persisted quietly, the silver eyes narrowed on her flustered face with a touch of steel in their depths.

'Because you don't belong in my world,' she said flatly, 'and they would know that.'

'I don't belong—?' She heard him swear very softly under his breath as he swung the big car out into the road, and she sat absolutely still before glancing from under her eyelashes at his face. It was very cold and angry.

'I didn't mean—'

'I don't want to know what you meant.' He cut across her voice before she could say more.

'Yes, but—'

'Shut up, Miriam.' It was said tightly, through clenched teeth. 'You really are the most—' He stopped abruptly and she saw him take a long pull of air before he relaxed slightly against the leather seat. ' "Bonny and blithe and good and gay",' he murmured grimly after one swift glance at her nervous face. 'I'm beginning to think they left out more than they put in.'

'But—'

'It will take us exactly ten minutes to reach the hotel I have in mind and I would very much appreciate quiet and tranquillity after the morning I've had, so if you don't mind....?' He glared at her once before concentrating on the road.

It took nearly a quarter of an hour as it happened, due to the inevitable roadworks that always sprouted around lunchtime, but as the Bentley turned off the main thoroughfare and through two enormous wrought-iron

gates into a small courtyard her stomach took a nose-
dive as she gazed at the impressive establishment in front
of them.

'Reece, I'm not dressed for somewhere like this,' she
began quickly, but he had left the car to walk round to
her door and her words were lost in the air.

'What did you say?' He helped her out, his hand firm
on her arm.

'I said—' She stopped abruptly. This was the sort of
place he frequented all the time, and he already knew
what she was wearing. If he was quite happy to bring
her here she would carry it off...somehow, but she just
knew that all the women would be in designer suits and
elegant, wildly expensive dresses.

They were.

'Your usual table, Mr Vance?' The head waiter appeared as though by magic as they walked into the restaurant and Reece smiled warmly.

'If it's free, Raimondo; we haven't booked, I'm
afraid.'

'I'm sure it's free, sir. If you and the young lady would
like to follow me...?'

Once seated at a secluded little table for two, she drew
breath and glanced about her. It really was a beautiful
place, she thought weakly, and the people... Surely that
was Geraldine Pace, the famous actress? She spotted
several more celebrities within seconds, and tried not to
gape. 'Now tell me this isn't better than a sandwich at
your desk?' Reece raised sardonic eyebrows and she tried
to muster an aplomb she didn't have.

'Just,' she admitted with a faint smile, glancing down
at the heavily embossed menu which the waiter had given
her once she'd been seated. There were no prices next
to the dishes listed, which spoke volumes about the cli-
entele, she thought weakly. What a place! If Mitch could
see her now. The thought reminded her of the old song
and her lips twitched in spite of herself.

'What?' Reece leant forward as he spoke. 'Tell me.'

'Tell you?' She gazed at him in surprise.

'What you were thinking just then that put that smile on your lips.'

'I—' She found that she was about to tell him, and stopped herself just in time. That note of command in his voice, the authority, was very hard to resist, and just at the moment her defences didn't seem to good. 'Why?' She gazed at him, the soft, discreet lighting in the restaurant turning his face into shadow, softening the harsh male lines. 'Why do you want to know?'

He shrugged as he sat back in his seat, his face sardonic. 'To answer a question with another question is a good ploy, Miss Bennett,' he said mockingly. 'I use it myself in business often.' He glanced round the restaurant, his eyes narrowed slits of silver. 'Everyone desperate to see and be seen,' he said softly, his gaze moving back to her face after a long moment. 'You find all this a little ridiculous, Miriam?'

'Ridiculous?' She stared at him in surprise and then shook her head quickly as she realised what he meant. 'I wasn't thinking about that, Reece—nothing so high-minded, I'm afraid.'

'No?' He sat up straighter, his eyes on her face. 'You like this, then, it appeals to you?'

She didn't quite know how to reply, and stared at him for a second before she decided that honesty was the best policy. 'I think it's wonderful—for a change,' she said politely. 'But I don't think I would want to live like this all the time. Not that it's without its appeal, but I think I must be more of a bread-and-butter girl than a soufflé type. I like to mess around in old jeans and take the dogs for a hike in the rain. Things like that, you know?' she finished awkwardly.

'Not really.' The dark face was quite expressionless.

'But this is really lovely—'

'For a change. Yes, I know,' he said wryly, with a small twist to his mouth that didn't speak of amusement.

She was immensely thankful that the waiter chose that moment to appear at Reece's side, head bowed deferentially, and after they had ordered she sipped tentatively at the cocktail the head waiter had brought to the table just after they had been seated.

'This is delicious,' she said, forcing a smile. 'And, Reece, I can't thank you enough for what you did. Whatever you say, I'm sure that man intended...' Her voice trailed away on a little shiver. 'Well, you know what he intended.'

'I know what he wanted you to *think* he intended,' Reece said calmly, 'but being hauled up on a rape charge is a sight more serious than threatening behaviour. The guy was trying to scare you, but I'll make sure they won't be back. You have my word on that, Miriam.' He smiled lazily. 'And now relax and enjoy your meal; that's an order.'

Relax? she thought incredulously. If she were seated opposite anyone else—*anyone* else—she might just be able to loosen up and unwind, let the beautiful surroundings and good food work their magic, but with Reece Vance within a hair's breadth? No chance.

The meal was delicious. The salmon canapés on their bed of green salad melted in the mouth, the grilled lamb cutlets with orange glaze sauce were cooked to perfection, and the cinnamon apple pie buried under its covering of thick double cream was out of this world.

Miriam couldn't help glancing round the other diners as she ate, noticing the languid, uninterested consumption of food in one or two areas accompanied by affected hand-waving as half-full plates were taken away by the ever attentive waiters, and the bottles of champagne being opened with monotonous regularity on certain tables. What posers!

The thought had popped into her mind of its own accord, but once in place she realised that it was absolutely right. There was one woman in particular who was enjoying being the centre of attention in her own little group, the men in the party leaning forward to catch her every word and the other women all sitting quietly with ingratiating smiles. She was sitting in profile to them, her body turned away, but from the little Miriam could see she was obviously outrageously beautiful in the delicate blonde way most men loved.

Reece had proved to be an attentive lunch companion, with a wickedly dry sense of humour, although he rarely smiled himself. There was a brooding quality to him, and Miriam couldn't rid herself of the impression that he was viewing the world as a stage, with the rest of them as performers, while he remained at a distance from them all, laconic and reserved. It was... disturbing.

'Reece, *darling*... You dreadful man! You were going to let me go without saying hello?' If anything could have underlined the difference between Reece's world and hers it was the woman bending over him so familiarly as she offered her lips for a kiss.

Miriam realised instantly that it was the woman she had noticed earlier and, close to, her beauty was even more impressive. She was tall and slim, her figure clothed immaculately in a chic black dress, and the thick, shining silver-blonde hair that had caught Miriam's eye earlier was coiled expertly into a glossy chignon at the nape of her neck. Her skin was flawless, her small nose perfect and, as she straightened and turned to Miriam, Miriam saw that the large, wide eyes were a deep jade-green and as clear as glass.

Reece had risen without comment and now gestured to Miriam, who remained seated. 'Miriam, I'd like you to meet an old friend of mine—Sharon Berkely-Smith. Sharon—Miriam.'

'How do you do?' The voice was cultured and soft and beautifully pitched, and as Miriam received the full force of the striking green eyes she felt almost dazed for a moment.

'Hello.' Miriam smiled politely as she met the blatant curiosity in the brilliant eyes. They swept over her face and figure with piercing sharpness before the woman turned back to Reece with a little sigh.

'Reece, darling, you really are the most annoying man. I thought you were going to ring me when you got Barbara's little muddle sorted?'

'I hardly think her wedding can be termed as a "little muddle" Sharon,' Reece said drily, 'and I haven't had the time.'

'Darling, you work too hard, you really do. We shall have you turning into a recluse if we aren't careful.' She turned to Miriam with a sweet smile that didn't touch the cool green eyes. 'But perhaps you are taking him in hand?'

'I...' Miriam was lost for words, and saw the fact register along with a certain degree of satisfaction in the lovely face in front of her.

'Miriam is taking care of some aspects of the wedding for me, Sharon,' Reece said coldly as he nodded to the other members of the party who had stopped a few feet away. 'And I think Bob and the others are waiting for you.'

'Oh, my marching orders?' She laughed gaily, but Miriam detected no amusement in the sound at all and suddenly realised, with mind-boggling amazement, that this elegant, exquisite, beautiful creature in front of her was actually put out at seeing Reece in her company. 'Goodbye, Miriam.' The clear green eyes were stony even as the curved red lips smiled a farewell. 'But perhaps I shall be seeing you again?'

'Possibly.' This was Reece at his most formidable, and Miriam was surprised that Sharon didn't wilt under the steely grey eyes, but the other woman just gave her light laugh as she reached up and kissed him again, her arms clinging round his neck just a trifle longer than necessary.

'I'll see you on Saturday, then, darling.' She turned gracefully on her heel as she spoke, the tall, slim body fluid. 'Half-past seven for eight o'clock and Daddy wants it formal; you know how Mother likes to dress up.'

'Goodbye, Sharon.' The dark voice was positively arctic now, but as Sharon disappeared in a whirl of silk and expensive perfume Miriam saw a satisfied tilt to the blonde head and with a sudden tightening in her throat heard the tinkling laugh as she reached the others.

'She's very beautiful.' She dragged her eyes from the departing group to Reece's face and saw that it was cool and bland, the grey eyes shuttered.

'Yes.' He gestured to her cup as the waiter appeared at their side again. 'More coffee?'

'No, thank you.' Suddenly there was a dead weight on her chest and a heavy thickness in her head. 'I really must get back to work; we're so busy.'

'As you wish.' He nodded to the waiter who returned with a slip of paper which Reece initialled as he helped her on with her coat. Of course. He'd have an account here. She glanced round the luxurious surroundings again and felt the weight get a little heavier. 'Come along.' He took her arm in his as they walked out of the restaurant and she was aware of several pairs of female eyes following their progress.

Once in the car, Reece said nothing beyond asking if she was warm enough as he adjusted the heater, and she sat quietly looking out of the window, her thoughts jumbled and confused as he drove swiftly back to the office.

Just before they turned into the small, run-down estate where the factory was situated Reece pulled the car off the road and through a gateway into a deserted, freshly ploughed field, and cut the engine before turning to face her, his eyes hooded.

'Sharon's family and mine have known each other for years,' he said flatly, his face grim. 'Our father's went to university together and had joint business interests for a good deal of their lives.'

'Oh.' She stared at him nervously, wondering why he was telling her all this.

'Sharon was born late in their lives, when they had given up all hopes of having children, and has consequently been spoilt outrageously,' he continued quietly. 'She tends to look on me as the older brother she never had.'

Older brother? Miriam almost choked. *Older brother?* Who was kidding whom? Whatever had prompted that little display in the restaurant, sisterly affection had had no place in it. She might be naïve and she might be unworldly, but did he really think that she was blind and stupid as well?

'Does she?' Miriam looked straight into the steady grey eyes and steeled herself not to lower her gaze. 'What has all this got to do with me?'

'I—' She saw a small muscle jerk by the side of his mouth as he stopped abruptly. 'Dammit, Miriam!' He had reached across and taken her in his arms before she'd realised his intention, but the second his mouth met hers there was nothing but sheer sensation in every curve and sinew of her body.

She had wanted him to kiss her. Almost from the first moment she had met him she had wanted to know what it would feel like for a man such as he to make love to her. She could hear her heartbeat surging into a faster tempo through the pounding in her ears, and a wild exhilaration that it was even better than she had imagined gripped her senses.

The lukewarm excitement she had felt on other occasions before she had brought matters to an abrupt halt had not prepared herself for the onslaught of Reece's mouth on hers. Those other men—boys, really—had slightly irritated her with their preoccupation with sex and she had begun to think that she must be frigid, but this... this was something else.

He moved her more comfortably into him without raising his head, and she could feel the thudding of his heart through his open jacket and the thin silk of his shirt, betraying his own excitement. As his tongue explored and tasted she clung to him helplessly, his big, powerful body and hard-muscled shoulders adding to the frissons of pleasure that were shivering through her and setting her blood on fire. He moved slightly to trace light, tantalising kisses in a little circle round her lips, and she almost moaned with the thrill of it.

This was crazy, madness. She pushed the thought away as his mouth moved to her throat, inflaming her senses still further before he took her mouth again in a kiss that was almost savage. His body was hard against hers, leaving her in no doubt as to the desire that she was firing in him, and as she returned his kiss with a frantic abandon she didn't recognise she knew that she was lost.

No wonder he was so cool and contained, so sure of himself; he must have women following him in droves. He was shatteringly, devastatingly good at this. She knew all that but it didn't stop her wanting him, needing more.

'Please...' She could hear her voice moaning, but couldn't have said what it was she was asking for. Reece seemed to know, moulding her into the powerful contours of his body as his fingers began an erotic massage over her taut back muscles that had her mouth opening in a silent gasp.

She had to stop this. The thought reverberated through the whirl of sensation. She had known this man barely twenty-four hours and she was allowing... 'Please stop.' She struggled slightly, her voice breathless. 'Please...'

He released her instantly, moving back into his own seat and raking his hand through his hair before turning to face her. Just for a moment she thought that he was as shaken as she was, but in the next instant, as she blinked, the look was gone from his face and, shockingly, the ice man was back, looking at her with cool, narrowed eyes.

'I'm sorry, Miriam.' He shook his head slightly as he turned to look out of the windscreen at the cold, bare world outside, the trees naked and black against the afternoon sky. 'I didn't intend that to happen. I didn't expect—' He stopped abruptly. 'I'm sorry,' he said again.

'I...' There was a lump in her throat constricting her breath, but it was the burning humiliation she felt that made speech impossible. He could sit there, cool and unmoved, while she was a shivering wreck? And she had thrown herself at him. She shut her eyes but the thought was still there.

She had sensed his surprise at her response even as he had kissed her, but she had wanted— She shook her head at her own thoughts. She had wanted him to make love to her. It was as simple as that. He would think that she was a tease, the sort of girl who egged a man on and then stopped at just the right moment.

'Look, I know you're inexperienced—'

'Please don't say anything,' she interrupted fiercely, her eyes burning with unshed tears. Inexperienced? So she hadn't even measured up to his other women anyway? Women like Sharon, maybe? Cool, sophisticated, blasé about their love affairs and life in general. She remembered her unskilled, raw response to his caresses and her skin burnt painfully. She had let him think that she was his for the taking and she had been—nearly.

'Listen—'

'Look, I don't normally act like this, Reece.' She spoke quickly, her face flaming. 'I don't know what came over me really. Too much alcohol, I think.' She tried a light laugh but it emerged as a strangled cough.

'You've had a hell of a day. I understand that.' His voice was soft with something. Pity? she thought frantically. Please, not pity. He didn't feel sorry for her, did he? 'I shouldn't have...'

'Yes, it must be the wine.' As he turned towards her she looked quickly out of the window. If she saw pity on his face that would be the last straw. Of course she couldn't begin to compare with the lovelies he normally associated with; he had probably only meant that kiss

as a comforting gesture, knowing that she was all at sea
from the incident before lunch. And she had practically
eaten him! She must have embarrassed him horribly...
Oh, hell.

'Miriam, I understand,' he said softly. 'Listen to me;
I didn't expect—'

This was getting worse. 'Can we just go now?' she
asked tightly.

'Not before I explain—'

'I don't want you to explain!' Did his other women
scream at him like a fishwife too? she wondered helplessly as he flinched at her shrill tone. 'I just want to go
back now. I can walk if you like; it's only a few yards
anyway.'

'*Miriam*...'

As he growled her name, the tone a warning that he
had come to the end of his tether, she flung open the
door before she had time to think and leapt out of the
car, only to find herself ankle-deep in thick red mud.

'You crazy female!' He glared at her as she stood hesi-
tating in the sticky dirt. 'Get back in this damn car. What
the hell do you think you're doing anyway?'

'I—' She stared at him as her thought processes spluttered and then died.

'Give me strength.' He put his hand to his brow as he
switched on the ignition. 'Satisfied? Now, get in.' He
was swearing softly under his breath as she rejoined him
in the car, and immediately her feet were off the ground
he reversed the Bentley violently across the few feet of
space into the gateway before she could even shut the
door properly, jerking to a halt as he checked his mirrors.
'I don't believe this is happening. I've never had a woman
react to me like this in all my life. What the hell do you
think I'm going to do to you anyway?'

She stared at him helplessly. He'd got it wrong; he'd
got it all wrong, but she couldn't find words to tell him
through the turmoil in her mind.

It took no more than a minute or two to reach the office where he screeched to a halt, the tyres protesting loudly. 'OK?' he snarled softly.

'Thank you,' she replied, with as much dignity as she could muster, clambering awkwardly out of the car, aware that she had left half the field on the pale gold carpet where her feet had rested.

'Haven't you forgotten something?' She turned at the sound of his voice. *'Again?'*

'Thank you.' She took the briefcase he was holding out to her with a scathing nod, hating him and hating herself for the ridiculous position that she was in. And it was all her fault. She could hardly believe that she, Miriam Bennett, had all but begged for him to take her out there in the open! And then to say no. And then to— She ground her teeth together in an agony of embarrassment as she turned and walked towards the office. The man's ego was jumbo size as it was, and she'd done nothing to deflate it. How he must be laughing at her.

The two vans were back and the Bentley had only been able to position itself in the entrance to the car park, but as she turned before stepping through the office she saw Mitch appear in the factory doorway and Reece leave the car where it was and walk across to him. She entered the office and shut the door firmly, walking across to the chair and collapsing on it before kicking off her mud-stained shoes.

What a day. *What a day.* And unless he was cancelling the contract with Mitch at this moment, and somehow she didn't think that Reece Vance was the sort of man to cut off his nose to spite his face, she was going to have to see him again at least a few times over the next two weeks. She shut her eyes tight against the thought.

Well, one thing was for sure. She tensed as she heard footsteps run across the path outside and then relaxed as Mitch burst into the office alone, his face anxious. She was *not* going to let Reece Vance within ten yards of her again. Not that he would want to anyway. With beauties like Sharon at his beck and call he wasn't exactly short of female companionship, and he'd made it perfectly clear how ridiculous he'd found her behaviour. And oh, hell, she couldn't blame him.

As she raised her head to answer the barrage of questions that Mitch was asking about the incident before lunch her face was resolute. She would never, ever put herself in such a vulnerable position again. For some reason she just couldn't trust her own body where Reece Vance was concerned, and it was painfully, devastatingly humiliating that he knew it too.

CHAPTER FOUR

REECE called just before she left the office that evening, to ask her to be at the house at eleven on Saturday morning, his voice terse and cool and his manner remote. 'Barbara has informed me she will be arriving about that time and I'm taking her out to lunch at twelve, so be prompt,' he added crisply.

'Of course, Mr Vance.' She was pleased how cool and professional her voice sounded when her insides were quivering like a jelly. 'How is your housekeeper?' she asked carefully, after a deep, silent breath.

'Fine.' There was a moment's pause. 'I understand the operation was a complete success and she will be allowed home after the weekend; she will obviously liaise with you from that point, OK? I'd like you to show her those schedules as soon as possible in case she can pick up on anything we may have missed. And the name is Reece, as you well know,' he added grimly.

'Right.' For the life of her she couldn't add to the monosyllable, and there was another brief pause before his voice sounded again, empty now of all expression.

'How are you feeling, Miriam?' For an awful moment she thought that he was referring to the incident in the car, before he followed on in the next breath, 'I explained everything to your brother and told him there should be two or three people around all the time. Not that I think there will be any trouble, I hasten to add, but it's safer to be cautious until I hear from this guy. I do *not* want you or any other woman there alone for the moment; do you understand me?'

Her hackles rose immediately at the authoritative, harsh tone. The cheek of it! Just who did he think he was anyway? This was *her* business and—

'I said, do you understand me?'

She was about to reply in the same abrupt, tight tone when the memory of how he had dealt with the two men without any thought for his personal safety sprang into her mind. He had helped her, and, not only that, he had taken on the problem that was Gregory himself in order that they wouldn't be troubled by his henchmen again. She was being churlish and petty in objecting to such a reasonable order, but it was the fact that it *was* an order, spoken in such autocratic, imperious tones, that had set her teeth on edge.

Nevertheless, she had every reason to be grateful to him, and she didn't like herself in this somewhat sour, querulous frame of mind. It was the antithesis of her nature. 'Yes, I understand you,' she responded quietly. 'And Mitch has already advised everyone of the full facts so there shouldn't be a problem.'

'Good.' The hard voice was a shade warmer. 'Goodnight, Miriam.'

'Goodnight.'

After she had replaced the receiver she sat for long minutes trying to regulate the beat of her heart, which had gone haywire the second she had heard his deep, cool voice. That skirmish in the car—it hadn't meant anything, not really. She shut her eyes very tight and clasped her hands together until the nails were biting into her skin. It had just been a kiss that had got out of hand for a moment or two, and after the morning she'd had, not to mention the champagne at lunch, it was hardly surprising. She would probably have reacted the same with almost anyone under the circumstances.

Her pounding heart challenged the lie but she shook her head determinedly, opening her eyes and picking up a piece of paper from her desk quickly as she heard Mitch's footsteps outside.

When her brother entered the office a second or two later he found her deep in work, brow wrinkled as she seemingly concentrated on a row of figures. 'Who was that on the phone just now?' he asked with perfunctory interest as he plumped down in his own chair. 'I heard it on the extension in the factory but you'd picked it up before I could get to it.'

'No problem.' She smiled brightly as she raised her head. 'It was Reece Vance arranging a meeting with his sister on Saturday.'

'Oh.' Mitch frowned slightly. 'He read me the Riot Act this afternoon,' he said slowly, his tone more than a little aggrieved. 'Wanted to know what I was doing leaving you alone here. Anyone'd think I knew those goons were going to come around! He seemed very concerned about you,' he added thoughtfully as his gaze roved over her suddenly hot cheeks. 'Unduly so, I thought.'

'Don't be silly.' She lowered her head, letting her hair swing in a veil over her burning face. 'He was here when it all happened and it was a bit scary, Mitch. I suppose he feels involved in some way, especially having seen those two men. They weren't the most pleasant of individuals.'

'Hmm.' Mitch continued to stare at her for a few moments more before busying himself with the heap of correspondence on his own desk. 'And that's it?' he asked after a minute or so. 'All this concern because he was here at the time? He took you to lunch, didn't he?' he added somewhat aggressively. 'Why?'

'*Why?*' She did raise her eyes at this point, to quell her brother with an icy glare. She had had more than enough of male assertiveness for one day, and if Mitch thought that he was going to intimidate her he could think again. 'Why not? I'm not answerable to you about who I choose to have lunch with, am I?'

'No.' Mitch's glance took in her lower lip, set in a distinctly pugnacious line. 'I just don't think Reece Vance is your type, that's all.'

'My "type"?' she squeaked disbelievingly as her voice rose in line with her temper. 'What on earth has my "type" got to do with anything? Not that I was aware I had one,' she added furiously. 'The guy felt sorry for me, for goodness' sake! I'd just been accosted by two beefy heavies and cried all over him, so I guess he didn't think he could just wave and leave. No doubt that's exactly what he would have liked to have done,' she added bitterly as Sharon's elegant image appeared in her mind's eye. 'We saw his girlfriend in the restaurant,' she said flatly, noticing the look of anxiety fade from Mitch's face with a trace of wry irony. 'And she is something else.'

'She is?' The relief on her brother's face would have been funny in any other circumstances.

'You'd better believe it,' Miriam said drily. 'So don't worry, big brother; the last person Reece Vance would go for is a little nobody like me. Satisfied?'

'I didn't think—' Mitch stopped abruptly at her raised eyebrows and grinned shamefacedly. 'Well, maybe I did at that. You're quite a looker yourself, Mim.'

'Pretty average on the whole.' She really couldn't continue this conversation without screaming and breaking something, Miriam thought tightly as her overstretched nerves twanged warningly. 'I think I'll get the rest of these recipes planned out at home after a long, hot bath. Can you give me a lift?'

'Sure thing.' Mitch gathered up some papers from his desk and stuffed them untidily into his briefcase. 'I'll do the same, I think. Sure you don't want to come back and have Mum spoil you a bit tonight?'

'Quite sure.' Any more fussing and she'd hit someone! 'I'm going to have a bath followed by beans on toast and then get on with some work.' She would never have thought that anything could sound so dull, she thought bleakly. 'Tell Mum I'll phone her later.'

And much later, as she lay in the comfortable darkness of her little bedsit with sleep a million miles away, she found herself thinking the same thought again as she reviewed her life to date.

It was all work and no play, she thought flatly, and had been for some years, but that had never worried her before, so why now? She was more than content with her career, she loved her little home, she had plenty of good friends... So what was wrong suddenly? She twisted irritably in the warmth of the bed and pulled the pillow over her head in an effort to stop her racing thoughts.

That nasty little incident with Gregory's hired thugs had unnerved her, that's all, she thought firmly. Brought the darker side of life into sharp focus for a while. By tomorrow she would be her happy-go-lucky self again, ready for anything. She *would*. She gritted her teeth and applied her considerable will-power to emptying her mind ready for sleep. Reece Vance meant nothing to her. *Absolutely nothing*, she repeated to herself firmly, before falling promptly to sleep.

It was pouring with rain when she drew up outside Reece's house at exactly eleven o'clock on Saturday morning, the icy droplets mixed with small, chilled flakes of snow. The sky was heavy and laden, the very air grey with a gloomy dark rawness that seeped into every nook and crevice, but as Miriam ran quickly up the steps to the house, red hair glowing and face alive with vitality, she seemed the very essence of spring to the tall dark man watching her from one of the windows.

She had dressed carefully that morning in a dark red jumper that exactly matched the unusual shade of her hair, teaming it with a full, long charcoal-grey skirt in thick wool with matching boots. Swinging gold loops in her tiny ears and a determined smile on her face completed the picture, and now, as she shrugged her heavy coat off and followed the small maid into the drawing room, she turned the smile up to full wattage when she saw Reece and a tall dark woman sitting having coffee. Reece Vance intimidate her? *Never*.

'I see you managed to get here in that rust-bucket.' Reece glanced across at her without a glimmer of a smile on his harsh face. 'Are you sure it's safe to drive, incidentally?'

'Reece!' His sister's shocked exclamation of protest was lost as Miriam slanted her eyes and prepared to do battle, her apprehension at facing him again after that disastrous afternoon vanishing in a puff of sheer anger.

'Of course,' she answered icily, her face straightening as she came to a halt in the middle of the room, hands on hips. 'It may look antiquated but it more than serves its purpose. We can't all drive darn great Bentleys,' she added tightly before she could stop herself.

'Pity,' he drawled slowly. 'For other road-users when you're about, that is... Now, Barbara, this is Miriam; Miriam meet my sister.'

'Hi.' The other woman had risen and now extended a slim hand to Miriam, her smile warm and friendly. 'Don't take any notice of Reece, will you? His bark has always been worse than his bite.'

'Really?' Miriam smiled back before glancing at Reece, her face adequately expressing all she didn't say. 'I can't say either action particularly appeals.'

Barbara was very like her handsome twin, with the same thick dark hair and startling silver-grey eyes, but the feminine genes had softened and mellowed Reece's hard male features into something quite beautiful in his sister, Miriam reflected silently as the two women shook hands.

'He was a difficult child and a difficult teenager and is now a supremely difficult man,' Barbara continued cheerfully with a sidelong glance at her brother, who was viewing the two women silently with cool, narrowed eyes, his face sardonic. 'Impossible to deal with.'

'When you've quite finished...' Reece indicated for Miriam to be seated as he fixed his sister with a steely glance that seemed to have no effect at all. 'We're here to finalise the details of your wedding, not to discuss my attributes—or lack of them,' he added drily. 'Now, Miriam, coffee?'

'Thank you.' Now that the rage was ebbing she was horrified at the effect he was having on her equilibrium but, dressed as he was in black denims and a black silk shirt, she was having a job to concentrate on anything other than her hormones. She forced herself to turn to Barbara with a shaky smile. 'Not long to wait until the big day.'

'Don't remind me.' The other woman groaned softly. 'I couldn't believe it when Reece phoned and told me the other catering firm were in police custody! I almost considered taking their case so I could get them out on bail in time for my wedding.' She grinned ruefully. 'And then poor Mrs Goode breaking her ankle.'

'Miriam?' As Reece handed her the coffee she nodded her thanks, glancing at him for the merest moment, but it was enough to set her heart pounding. He was too attractive for comfort and, this close, all she could think about was how it had felt when he'd kissed her. And the feel of that big, hard body pressed into hers. And the smell of him. And—

'I'll leave you two to it.' He picked up his own cup and walked lazily across the room, his body moving with relaxed, easy power. 'I'll be in my study, if you want me.'

'We won't.' Barbara softened her words with a warm smile as he turned and raised sardonic eyebrows before leaving the room. 'Now, Miriam, do you mind if I see what you've got planned?' she asked eagerly as she settled down in her chair, her eyes bright with interest.

The next half-hour sped by in a whirl of lists and notes, but at the end of it the two women were chatting like old friends. 'You've done absolute wonders at such short notice,' Barbara sighed gratefully as Miriam packed away the last of the papers and clicked her briefcase shut. 'I wouldn't have a clue where to start with anything remotely domestic, I'm afraid.'

She wrinkled her small, pert nose at Miriam, her face candid. 'I don't know where all my nest-making and womanly instincts went in that area, but I rather think another little girl baby ended up with a double dose when I was born! I can just about manage to boil an egg, but I've ruined three or four saucepans doing that simple task because I always forget and let the water boil dry— normally because I've got my nose stuck in a law book or something,' she added ruefully. 'I'm hopeless.'

'So you and your future husband will eat out of tins or at the local restaurant?' Miriam said laughingly. The other woman's candour was infectious.

'Oh, there's no problem in that direction,' Barbara answered happily. 'Craig's the most marvellous cook. Wait till you see him, Miriam! He's six foot four and the most gorgeous thing on two legs and *definitely* all male.' Her voice lowered suggestively as she winked saucily. 'But he can whip up a meal for four out of nothing and restore order to the disgusting clutter I call a home within minutes. We've already decided I'll be the one who earns the money and he'll stay home with the kids—when they arrive, of course,' she added longingly. 'I've never really wanted a family before, but the minute I met Craig I wanted his baby so bad I almost propositioned him then and there!'

She gazed dreamily at Miriam, looking most unlawyerlike. 'I've been searching for this man all my life without knowing it and it just amazes me he feels the same. We're like two halves that fit into a perfect whole.' The slight throb in the other woman's voice told Miriam that she was absolutely genuine. 'I'd made up my mind when I was still at school that I was going to be a career woman and that marriage was *definitely* out of the question, and then Craig came into my life and that was that.' She sighed happily. 'He's just gorgeous.'

'Lucky old you.' Miriam wondered how to word what she wanted to say and spoke carefully. 'And Reece knows how you feel about each other?'

'Reece?' Barbara sat straight and wrinkled her nose irritably. 'Oh, my brother is a typical orthodox male. I can't talk to him, Miriam, I really can't. I know he disapproves of Craig—not so much by what he *has* said but more by what he hasn't! He hasn't even met him properly yet, just once at a crowded party, where everyone had had too much to drink and everything went wrong.

'Craig had come across from Australia that day after visiting his parents, and had rushed to the party from the airport because I wanted him to. He had the most awful jet lag, poor lamb, and went to sleep in a corner of the sofa in spite of the noise and chaos. Some tarty blonde draped herself all over him—she was out for the count on cider—and Reece arrived at that moment and got totally the wrong impression.'

'I see.' Miriam looked the other woman straight in the eyes. 'Don't you think it'd put Reece's mind at rest if you explained all that?'

'I shouldn't have to.' Suddenly the resemblance between brother and sister was striking as Barbara's mouth set in a hard, stubborn line. 'He should trust my choice; he knows I'm no fool.' She shook her head testily. 'And I'm thirty-five years old, for crying out loud! I don't have to explain everything to my brother, do I?'

'No, of course not,' Miriam agreed soothingly. 'But he loves you—'

'I know.' Barbara nodded despondently. 'And I love him too. He's the only person in the world who has ever really cared a jot about me, until I met Craig; I think he kept me sane when I was little—' She suddenly seemed to realise that she had said more than she'd intended and shut her mouth with a little snap, the same cool, aloof mask that habitually clothed her brother's face settling over Barbara's like a veil.

Miriam opened her mouth to reassure Reece's sister that she understood at the same time as the door opened and Reece stood framed in the doorway, his silver eyes narrowing immediately on the two women's faces.

'Finished?' he asked abruptly.

'Just,' Barbara answered quickly as she stood up, smoothing her beautifully cut dress over her slim hips. 'You've found an absolute life-saver here, you know.'

'Yes, I do.' There was something in the deep male voice that caught Miriam's attention, but then he continued in the usual cool, bland tone and she told herself that she must have imagined the husky warmth that she thought she had detected.

'I wondered if you'd like to join us for lunch, Miriam?' he asked expressionlessly as he watched her rise to her feet just as the telephone began to ring on the table at Barbara's side. His sister reached across and listened to the voice on the other end as Miriam stared at Reece in surprise, the sudden invitation numbing her mind, and then Barbara stretched out her arm to her brother, the receiver dangling between her fingertips.

'Sharon,' she said briefly. 'For you.' Her fine eyebrows rose cynically as Reece took the telephone from her with an irritated frown.

'Hello, Sharon.' Reece's voice was cool. 'What can I do for you?'

Now there's a silly question, Miriam thought with painful humour as she watched his hard profile. She knew exactly what the beautiful blonde would like Reece to do for her!

'Yes, seven-thirty for eight; you did mention it,' Reece said quietly into the phone. 'And would you tell your father I shall be bringing the reports we were looking at in the week? They're all complete now,' he continued as Barbara raised wicked eyebrows at Miriam.

'Have you met our sweet little Sharon yet?' she whispered sarcastically as she drew Miriam to one side.

'Yes,' Miriam responded cautiously. Reece's sister was not at all what she had expected. 'Last week, actually.'

'Poisonous little flower, isn't she?' Barbara drawled matter-of-factly, without a shred of malice in her voice. 'I don't think I know of one woman under the age of sixty who gets on with her, she is so openly hostile to her own sex.'

She sighed heavily as she glanced across at her brother. 'But of course the men all love her; they really don't seem to be able to see through her at all. She loathes me,' she added with great satisfaction. 'I've always taken it as an enormous compliment. I can't think of a worse indictment than to have Sharon's approval.'

'I understand the two families are close,' Miriam said diplomatically, without venturing an opinion on Sharon herself. It was one thing for Reece's sister to dislike his girlfriend but quite another for his temporary employee to criticise his choice in women.

'Well, the two sets of parents certainly were,' Barbara replied quietly. 'But Reece and I were never at home when we were children. Since our parents died Reece has had more to do with Sharon's father on a business level and I think they get on quite well. Sharon is ten years younger than us so it's only been in the last few years she's really made her presence known.' She glanced at her brother as he wound up the call, his voice terse and his face remote. 'I think she gets on Reece's nerves half the time.'

What about the other half? Miriam thought miserably as she pictured the blonde's beautiful face and figure, hoping that her thoughts didn't show on her face as Reece turned abruptly to join them. 'Well?' He looked straight at Miriam. 'Are you joining us for lunch?'

The image of Sharon was suddenly so real that Miriam could have reached out and touched her and she shook her head quickly, keeping her voice cool but pleasant. 'No, thanks, but it's kind of you to ask. My mother is expecting me.'

'No problem.' The silver-grey eyes were narrowed on her face, as though they wanted to read her mind, and it was with a real effort of will that she broke the piercing gaze, turning and walking to the door as she made her goodbyes to Barbara.

Several mortifying minutes later, when she had tried all the tricks she knew to start the car and was peering despondently under the bonnet, Reece appeared at her side, his face a study in blankness. '"Antiquated" was the word you used, I think?' he drawled lazily as his head joined hers over the car's insides.

She might have known that he would rub it in, she thought furiously, longing to give the side of the car a massive kick. How could it do this to her? Here, of all places? There was no justice. 'It doesn't like wet weather,' she said tightly as she concentrated on peering at the engine in the murky light, vitally aware of the big dark body next to her, clothed in a black leather jacket that sat on the broad shoulders in a manner guaranteed to make any red-blooded female take a second look.

'Who does?' He stood back a pace, folding his arms as he stared at her in the icy drizzle. 'You're getting very wet,' he added conversationally.

'I know.' She glared at him in exasperation. If he hadn't got anything better to say he could clear off back indoors, she thought angrily.

'Do you know how that works?' he asked softly after a long, tense moment when she just knew that he had read her mind. The knowledge was there in the dark glitter of his narrowed eyes and straight, hard set to his mouth.

'Usually.' She straightened as a trickle of very cold water dripped stealthily down the space between her coat and neck and willed herself not to shudder. 'I took a course in car maintenance a couple of years ago.'

'Did you now?' She had seen the flash of surprise in his grey eyes before he could hide it and felt enormously pleased that she had managed to pierce that control just a little.

'Yes.' She smiled sunnily, knowing that it would annoy him. 'It seemed like a good idea at the time and has got me out of quite a few difficulties with this old girl.' She tapped the side of the car gently. 'But not this time, I'm afraid. Could I use your—?'

'I'll give you a lift.' He had interrupted her before she could finish and she kept the smile in place with sheer determination.

'Phone?' she continued pointedly. 'I can get a taxi and arrange for this to be collected—'

'No need.' He'd done it again, she thought tightly. 'I'll give you a lift to wherever you're going—Barbara and I were just leaving anyway—and arrange for someone to look at the car and drive it to your house some time tomorrow. OK?'

'But garages don't work on a Sunday,' she said quickly, 'and I can sort it out myself. There's really no need for you to bother about it.'

'No bother.' A glimmer of a smile touched the hard face for a second. 'And they *will* work on a Sunday if I want them to.' The quirk to his mouth disappeared as he moved closer, looking down at her as the droplets of rain sat in her silky red hair like tiny diamonds. 'Why don't you like me?' he asked expressionlessly. 'Do I frighten you?'

She couldn't answer, the pounding of her heart and sudden dryness in her throat rendering her dumb as she looked up into the dark, cool face. He seemed very big and very powerful as he reached out and drew her, almost casually, into his arms, his chin resting on the top of her head as he nuzzled her wet hair with his chin.

'I should imagine you are the type of person who can get on with anyone,' he said thoughtfully over her head. 'But with me there is a definite withdrawal every time I so much as look at you. Why?'

His arms tightened a fraction and she forced herself to stand absolutely still as the intoxicating smell of expensive aftershave on clean male skin set her pulse racing like an express train. Her senses were alive as they had never been before, her nerves aware of the lean male body in a way that was positively wanton, and she was terrified that he would sense her response—sense it and capitalise on it.

He was dangerously threatening to her peace of mind, she told herself desperately, whether he was being coldly patronising, coolly mocking or menacingly tender—like now. This sort of thing meant nothing to him, she knew that. With women like Sharon dancing attendance she had no chance at all, so why, *why* did her body have to react like this?

'No answer?' he asked softly. 'Look at you now, rigid as a board. Do you think I'm going to drag you off into the bushes and have my wicked way with you or something? It's hardly the weather for such games, is it?' he added mockingly.

'Don't be ridiculous.' She managed to jerk away, her cheeks scarlet, as her wits returned with his mockery. 'I just don't play the sort of "games" that you obviously indulge in, that's all.'

'It was purely a figure of speech, Miriam.' One dark eyebrow rose satirically upwards at her angry face. 'And, for the record, I don't play games either. Anything I do, I do for real.'

'You know what I mean.' She backed away as she spoke, feeling safer with a metre or two of air between them.

'Unfortunately I think I do.' He crossed his arms and stared down at her like a great black hunter sighting its prey. 'You seem to have the impression that I am—how can I put it without being too indelicate?—little better than a stud stallion.'

'Well, if that's being delicate I'd hate to hear you when you're speaking frankly.' She blinked at him as a tiny star of snow settled on the eyelashes of one eye, and rubbed her wet face warily.

'You're getting soaked.' He suddenly seemed to remember her bedraggled state. 'Come on; come into the house for a minute and dry off while I phone the garage.

At the very least you can allow me the privilege of running you to your mother's,' he continued drily, 'when you are single-handedly saving Barbara's great day.'

She eyed him suspiciously; the words had sounded very much like an insult wrapped in the bright paper of a compliment, but he stared back at her innocently, a small smile playing round the hard mouth.

'Even the most dissolute of rogues is allowed to be noble on occasions, surely?'

'And you think you fit that description? Of dissolute rogue?' she asked sweetly as she allowed him to take her arm and lead her back towards the house.

'No.' He stopped abruptly and turned her into the length of him as all amusement left his face. 'I don't, but you sure as hell do.' And then he kissed her. Hard. With more than a shred of anger mixing with the hot hunger as his mouth ravished hers. And although she knew that it was madness, that she would regret it bitterly as soon as she was free of his arms, she kissed him back.

'Miriam, Miriam...' He cupped her face with his hands, his kiss more penetrating now as his tongue plundered the sweetness of her mouth in fierce, darting movements that caused the blood to run wild in her veins. And just for a second, before reason asserted itself, she longed to melt into the body of this dangerous, hard individual and drown in his caress. 'So sweet,' he murmured against her parted lips. 'So defenceless...'

Defenceless? If he had struck her she couldn't have reacted more violently as she wrenched herself out of his arms, her face flaming. And what exactly did that mean, as if she didn't know? she asked herself furiously. Substitute naïve, simple—stupid, even. But she *wasn't* stupid and she didn't trust him, not an inch, and, what was more, she was at least worldly-wise enough to recognise that the only possible interest he could have in someone like her was a brief flaring of physical attraction that would die as swiftly as it was born.

He wasn't her type and she certainly wasn't his. One look at Sharon had made that little fact abundantly and painfully clear, but she *was* a change from his normal diet of cool, elegant, sophisticated women of the world, and therefore something of a novelty. There was no reason why the knowledge should hurt so much. No reason at all.

'Could I please just use the phone?' she asked tightly as she gathered the remnants of her tattered pride into place. 'I think I'd prefer that to the payment you obviously expect for a lift.' It was unforgivable, but just at that moment the need to prove that she was mistress of her own emotions, as cool and capable and independent as he was, was paramount. Inside she felt crushed and buffeted by a hundred different sensations but he mustn't guess—he mustn't ever guess.

'Payment?' In the split second before his face became a blank mask, the hard jaw set and cold, she saw pure, undiluted rage in the silver-grey eyes and it was frightening. He swore once, softly but with great purpose, and then took hold of her arm in a punishing grip as he whisked her into the house, almost lifting her off her feet in his temper. 'Sit!' As he threw her into a big easy chair in the drawing room the tone was exactly the same as one might use to a disobedient dog, and she reared up at the sound.

'How dare you—?'

'Not a word—*not a word*, Miriam.' He glared at her one more time before leaving to return almost immediately with a massive, fluffy bath towel which he flung at her with more force than was necessary. 'Dry yourself,' he said tightly, 'while I get Barbara down here. And then you will get into my car—with my sister as chaperon, I hasten to add—and I will take you to wherever you want to go.'

It sounded as if he could suggest somewhere that was very hot and very unpleasant, she reflected silently as she did exactly as she was told, rubbing her dripping wet hair weakly as she contemplated the rigid fury in his back as he strode from the room. Why on earth had she provoked him? she asked herself flatly.

It was a question that continued to burn in the back of her mind all the way to her mother's house, even as she kept up a light conversation with Barbara, who chatted away in the back of the car quite oblivious to the tension between Miriam and her brother. She had allowed him to get under her skin, and at the very least it was grossly unprofessional and at the worst— She caught her lip between her teeth and bit down hard. At the worst it was suicidal, she thought miserably as she glanced at the dark, grim profile.

As they drew up outside her mother's neat little detached house with its trim garden she forced a smile on her lips and turned to Reece, only to find that he had left the car and was opening her door, his face cold. 'You'd better give me your address,' he said abruptly. 'For the car to be returned.'

'There's really no need...' She quailed under his ferocious glare and gave him the address in a small voice.

'Thank you,' he said with infinite sarcasm as he turned to walk back round the bonnet of the car.

'Reece?' Her voice halted him in his tracks as he glanced at her troubled face. 'I didn't mean it, about the payment.' She stared at him as he didn't move, his face perfectly still. 'It was a cheap jibe and I apologise, but I'd still rather sort the car out myself,' she added with a raising of her small chin.

'The car is on my property; I know someone who will deal with it straight away so you won't be inconvenienced too much; it's simpler,' he said in a monotone. 'And the apology is accepted.'

'Good.' She found herself smiling at his angry face in spite of herself, sensing that her apology had taken him by surprise.

He stared back at her for a long moment and then she saw a glimmer of a smile touch the straight mouth. 'Good

and gay,' he murmured to himself as he walked round
the car, his face sardonic. 'I'd have preferred bad and
gay, personally. I'll see you Monday morning, Miriam.'
And then he was gone in a swirl of gleaming pale gold
metal as Barbara waved cheerfully out of the car window.

She was at home later that night when Frank rang, curled
up in front of the small gas fire in her bedsit as she
watched an old movie on TV and struggled to put every
thought of Reece Vance out of her mind.

'Hi, Mim.' Frank's voice was warm as he called her
by the old nickname he had used ever since she'd been
a baby. 'How's Bennett and Bennett, then?'

'Fine.' She smiled into the phone. 'Thanks for putting
us onto the Vance job, Frank, it's worth a mint.'

'Thought so.' Frank's voice expressed his satisfaction.
'Reece Vance might be a difficult man to deal with, but
he is fair. I was really ringing to see if all went well; it
obviously did, then?'

'We've got the job, if that's what you mean,' Miriam
said carefully. 'I met his sister today and got all the loose
ends tied up.'

'Barbara?' Frank was approving. 'Nice lady, isn't she?
Never thought she'd ever get married, though; didn't
think either of 'em would ever tie the knot. You know
they're twins?'

'Yes, Reece told me.' There was a blank little silence
at the other end of the phone and then Frank spoke, his
voice slightly hesitant.

'Reece? You're on first-name terms, then?'

'Yes.' She wrinkled her brow at the phone. 'Anything
wrong in that, Frank?'

'Not at all.' His voice was too hearty and he seemed
to realise it too, because he had moderated the tone when
he next spoke. 'The thing is, Mim, I know the ladies
tend to be attracted to the guy, and I wouldn't like to
think—' He stopped abruptly. 'That is...I was your
father's best friend, Mim, and I promised him I'd always

look out for the family if anything ever happened to him.'

'And you have,' she said softly. 'In lots of ways.'

'It's just that Reece Vance is the sort of guy most people would rather have as a friend than an enemy,' Frank continued slowly. 'Know what I mean? He can be ruthless in business, and from what I've heard he's pretty lethal in his personal life too. He works hard and plays hard but he never gets attached to anyone—keeps himself pretty remote. He's broken quite a few hearts in his time, I understand, although he makes it clear he operates on a strictly no-strings-attached policy, but you know what women are—always thinking they can change a man.'

'Frank?' She interrupted quickly as he paused for breath. 'Why are you telling me all this?'

'Why?' There was another brief pause. 'No reason, Mim; just filling you in on a bit of background, that's all.'

'I'm only doing the catering for his sister's wedding,' Miriam said softly. She closed her eyes tightly.

'Yes, fine...' Frank was clearly embarrassed now. 'And I know you'll do an excellent job too; you and Mitch have worked like beavers these last few years.' He hesitated and then spoke again, his voice resolute, as though he had nerved himself to say all he had planned. 'I just wanted you to understand, to avoid getting the wrong impression, that's all.'

'The wrong impression?' she asked quietly as she opened her eyes.

'Reece Vance is the kind of man who doesn't like women—' Frank's voice stopped abruptly. 'I don't mean he doesn't *like* women—that he likes men,' he added hastily. 'I mean— Oh, hell, Mim, you know what I mean.'

'That he uses them for one thing and one thing only?' she asked softly as she felt a physical pain in her heart region.

'Well, that's the way it seems.' Frank was clearly wishing that he had never phoned. 'Of course I could be wrong, but I don't think so. Anyway, congratulations on getting the job, Mim, and I'll probably see you at your mother's some time soon. Take care.'

'And you, Frank.'

She sat looking at the phone for some minutes after the call had ended, her heart heavy and her head spinning. Well, she had known, hadn't she? she asked herself sharply, biting back the urge to cry with savage intensity. He was the original loner—that much had been crystal-clear from the first moment she had set eyes on him. And of course the women would flock around him.

She shook her head blindly as she stood up and walked over to the breakfast bar, switching on the electric kettle and spooning coffee and sugar into one of her china mugs. The same fascination that had gripped her would almost certainly affect the rest of the female population, she told herself grimly as she poured boiling water onto the dark granules of coffee and inhaled the fragrant odour before adding milk. She hadn't expected to be the only one attracted to him, after all.

She continued to talk to herself in fits and starts for the rest of the evening, and woke early the next morning feeling as though she hadn't slept. The winter sky was a sea of silver and gold in the clear light just after dawn and she sat for over an hour watching the slowly changing cloud formation as she ate her breakfast of toast and marmalade.

'Work, work, work.' She glanced across at the pile of files that she had brought home and felt a sudden surge of rebellion. She needed a day out in the fresh air to restore her equilibrium, and that was exactly what she was going to have. She rang her mother just after nine and asked her to have the dogs ready, after checking that Mitch had driven home in one of the company vans the night before. Then she set out on a brisk walk to her mother's house, which took exactly an hour through the deserted streets.

After loading the delighted animals into the back of the van she set out for a country park that she had visited in the summer, arriving just after eleven and spending a wonderful day tramping through the wooded hills and hollows, to arrive back at her mother's house in time for tea with a van full of exhausted and happy dogs, mind and body restored to their normal stability.

She ate a huge meal before plodding back through the dusk-filled streets, refusing Mitch's offer of a lift home with unusual firmness but feeling more than a little glad as she turned into the street where her bedsit was situated. Her legs suddenly seemed to have gained the consistency of solid lead.

Her car was parked outside the house. As she opened the door to her room she found a note on the floor, which had obviously been pushed under the door. 'Sorry I missed you.' As her eyes fastened on the strong male writing she felt her heart begin to pound. 'Mechanic fixed the car with no trouble and I thought I'd deliver it myself, see how the other half get about.' She could just imagine how he'd written that, tongue-in-cheek and loving the dig. 'Keys are with the delightful blonde girl next door, who very kindly gave me a cup of coffee before I began my weary trek home. See you tomorrow.' There was no signature but she didn't need one.

He'd come here? She glanced round her tiny home and sat down very suddenly. Why? He could easily have let the mechanic deliver the car. What time had he come? Had he expected to spend some time with her? She felt a rush of intense disappointment before shaking her head violently. Don't be stupid, she told herself sharply. This didn't mean a thing—not a thing.

She glanced again at his handwriting. So he thought that Charlotte was delightful did he? And she could just imagine what the tall, slim blonde next door had thought of Reece!

She found that she was clenching the paper tightly in her fist and forced herself to relax her hand, shaking her head at her own thoughts as she did so. He was her temporary employer, that was all, and after what Frank had said she had no excuse to imagine anything more. He might be prepared to have a brief liaison with her, but that would be all it would mean for him. And she wasn't going to be one of his ships that passed in the night. No way.

She stood up, her legs her own again now, and prepared to collect her keys from Charlotte and answer the host of questions that would undoubtedly come her way at the same time.

CHAPTER FIVE

MIRIAM arrived at Reece's house with her two assistants just before nine in the morning to find that he had already left for the office.

'Mr Vance said I had to give you the keys to the extension entrance,' Jinny the maid informed her after she had knocked on the front door. 'There's a door at the far end of the corridor which makes it nice and easy for delivering stuff to the kitchens and he said for you to come and go as you please. You know you can get through to the main part of the house through the hall?'

'Yes. Thank you.' Miriam smiled at the young girl who grinned back cheerfully.

'Mrs Goode is coming home today,' she said happily. 'Mr Vance is collecting her before lunch.'

'That's good.' Miriam nodded and smiled again as she turned and walked back to the van, in which was packed a whole host of supplies from the wholesalers they used. She hadn't got time to stand and chat today; the work schedule was going to be tight as it was.

After parking the van just outside the extension entrance on the tarmac pull-in, she helped Vera and Dave unload and set up in the kitchens and then the three of them started work in earnest. The up-to-date equipment and beautiful surroundings made cooking a joy, and she was just taking a batch of golden quiches out of one of the ovens when some sixth sense made her glance towards the door. Reece was standing in the doorway looking at her, his dark face expressionless.

'Hi.' He nodded to the other two as he introduced himself and shook hands before turning to her again. 'Mrs Goode is home and I thought it might be an idea for you to meet her now; I want her to rest this afternoon.'

'Of course.' She was shocked by how the sight of him had affected her and hoped, desperately, that he hadn't noticed her agitation. 'Thank you for delivering the car yesterday,' she added stiffly as she slipped out of her enormous work apron and pushed a stray strand of hair off her face. 'It was nice to be able to drive to work and pick up the van.'

'No problem.' He walked over to the door without looking at her again. 'Ready?' He didn't speak as they walked down the corridor and through the big hall; indeed, he didn't seem conscious of her presence, Miriam thought silently as she followed him into the main part of the house, clutching the file that she had brought with her.

'Reece?' She stopped him just as they were about to enter the drawing room. 'How much do I owe you?'

'Owe me?' He stared at her in surprise.

'For the car,' she said quietly. 'I'm sure you had to pay the man and I don't expect—'

'Oh, forget that.' He shook his head almost irritably. 'It was nothing.'

'But I must pay you—'

'Don't be silly, Miriam; I told you, it was nothing.' He took her arm as though the matter was finished. 'Now come and meet Mrs Goode—'

'Reece, I *always* pay my way.' She moved to stand in front of him as he went to open the door, her small face determined and her violet eyes very serious. 'I wouldn't feel comfortable otherwise.'

'We'll see about it later.' Now there was a definite note of irritation colouring the deep voice. 'I might have known you would be the only female of my acquaintance who would insist on refusing a gift,' he added tightly. 'Most of them have no such scruples.'

'It wasn't a gift. Not in the traditional sense anyway,' she added quickly as she felt the words sounded un-

grateful. 'And it was very kind of you to arrange everything, without paying for it too.'

Most of them, she thought bleakly. Most of them?

'I'm a kind man.' Before she realised what he was
doing he had kissed the tip of her nose lightly and moved
her to one side. 'As I'm sure you will appreciate once
you get to know me better,' he added enigmatically as
he opened the door and ushered her through.

Mrs Goode was older than she had expected, and
frailer, but it was Reece's attitude to the elderly housekeeper that surprised Miriam the most. She had expected— She hadn't known what she'd expected, she
thought silently as she watched Reece fetch the small
woman a cup of tea from the tray that Jinny had just
brought in and adjust the rug on her knees; but this
gentleness that he was displaying was a definite jolt to
the picture she had began to form in her mind's eye.
And Mrs Goode clearly worshipped the very ground her
employer walked on.

'Such a silly thing to do,' she said ruefully, with a
small shake of her bird-like head as she gestured to her
ankle which was heavily encased in plaster. 'I must be
getting old.'

'It's nothing to do with age and you know it.' Reece
smiled at the older woman as he spoke and something
twisted in Miriam's chest as she saw the warmth between
them. 'Sheer stubbornness as usual. I'd told you and
told you not to carry too much when you go down those
stairs; Jinny can do all of that.'

'Oh, away with you.' Mrs Goode flapped her hand at
him and Miriam's mouth opened slightly with surprise.
'I'm too old a bird to change the habits of a lifetime
now.'

They sat for some minutes discussing the schedule and
lists that Miriam had brought to show the housekeeper,
who expressed her approval of Miriam's plans with
wholehearted enthusiasm. 'Lovely, my dear.' Miriam
noticed the slightly strained look in the housekeeper's

eyes and it appeared that Reece did too, because he stood up suddenly, his voice firm as he glanced at the older woman's white face.

'Bed for you.' He smiled at Mrs Goode gently. 'I'm going to help you upstairs before I go, and there you stay for the rest of the day.'

'But there's so much to do.' The elderly woman peered up at him anxiously. 'And Barbara won't be able to help.'

'It's all in hand, Mrs Goode,' Miriam said carefully, not wishing to step on the older woman's toes but realising that she needed to rest. 'If I run into any problems I'll give you a call, if I may—pop and see you. But there are several things that can only be done in the last two or three days so I was hoping you'd be able to do those when you're feeling better, and perhaps oversee the temporary staff.'

'I'm getting you a wheelchair tomorrow, just for a couple of weeks,' Reece added firmly, 'and you'll be able to skitter about in that to your heart's content, but just for today do as you're told and stay in bed, would you?' He helped his housekeeper to her feet and supported the thin little body with a hand round her waist as Mrs Goode turned and smiled at Miriam.

'Goodbye, dear.' She patted Miriam's hand quietly. 'You're doing wonders, dear; well done.'

'It's my job.' Miriam smiled cheerfully.

'And such a lovely smile,' the old woman continued with the embarrassing candour of the elderly. 'Have you got a young man?'

'No, she's fancy-free,' Reece interposed, with a sardonic glance at Miriam's pink face. 'Married to her job, so I understand.'

It was clear that Mrs Goode wanted to say more, but Reece led her very firmly from the room as Jinny appeared to take the old woman's other arm, and Miriam sped off back to the kitchens with her face burning.

Vera and Dave had organised a quick snack and switched the coffee-pot on, but just as she took a big bite of her ham and tomato sandwich Reece appeared in the doorway to the kitchen. 'Could I have a word?' he asked grimly as she hastily swallowed and rose. 'In the flat?'

'Of course.' She followed him out into the corridor and into the small flat warily. What now?

'I just wanted to thank you for being so tactful with Mrs Goode,' he said surprisingly as he turned to face her in the bright little lounge. 'She's fretting about the arrangements but you put her mind at rest at the same time as making her feel useful.' The silver eyes narrowed on her clear face. 'You understand people quite well, don't you?'

'Some,' she said lightly. There was one within a hair's breadth who was a complete enigma if he did but know it.

'And I was going to suggest that at the end of the week, or maybe at the weekend, it might be a good idea for you to move in here,' he added quietly. 'With the amount of work that needs to be done it seems to make sense to be living on the job.'

'I—' It *did* make sense but somehow, without knowing why, the thought of actually living in his house made something hot and liquid trickle shiveringly down her spine. Stupid. Animal chemistry. Imagination. It was probably all of those things, but this feeling that made her catch her breath as she faced him wouldn't be denied. 'I'll see later; it might not be necessary,' she prevaricated uncomfortably, flushing as he laughed derisively.

'I'm not going to break the door down in the middle of the night,' he said with cool mockery. 'You'll be quite safe even if you are in the wolf's lair.'

'I never doubted that for a minute,' she said stiffly, her cheeks getting still hotter as he raised a disbelieving eyebrow before sauntering out of the room with a silent wave of his hand.

He had to be the most irritating, annoying man she had ever met in her life, she thought crossly as she closed

the front door to the flat and joined the others across
the corridor. But she wasn't going to think of him now;
there was too much to do. And too little time in which
to do it.

They worked hard all day, and when they left the house
just before six Reece still wasn't home. She dropped Vera
and Dave off and arrived back at the bedsit utterly
exhausted and longing for a relaxing hot bath. After an
hour's soak she felt a little more herself, and she fixed
a quick meal of cold meat and salad and ate it in her
dressing gown in front of the fire, flexing her toes in the
warmth from the gas jets now and again as she watched
TV.

She had just settled down to planning the time sheet
for the next day when Mitch rang. 'You'll never guess,
Mim.' Her brother's voice was both relieved and faintly
apprehensive. 'Reece Vance has paid off all the re-
maining debt with the garage and old man Gregory hasn't
made a murmur. We had all the papers through today,
so that's that little problem out of the way.'

'But—' She stopped abruptly. So now they were under
obligation to Reece financially. She didn't like that; she
didn't like it at all. 'What were the terms for paying Reece
back?' she asked carefully.

'I knew you'd ask that so I phoned him,' Mitch said
quickly. 'He insists he doesn't want a formal agreement;
we just pay him back what we can when we can, and he
made the point that he definitely doesn't want any
interest added. Not quite what you'd expect from an
astute businessman like him, is it?' her brother asked
wryly.

'No, it certainly isn't.' It had got them out of a bad
situation with Gregory, it was undeniably generous and
more than kind of him. So why was she finding it so
difficult to be pleased? she asked herself silently. What
was it, some sort of pride?

Sudden self-knowledge made her flush painfully. That was exactly it, she admitted slowly. He was extremely wealthy and, by his own admission, used to women who were inclined to take when they could and she wanted to be... different. She closed her eyes tightly as a hot dose of self-contempt burnt in her chest. She had wanted him to respect her, admire her principles, know that she wasn't like all the others.

She shook her head at her own stupidity. Who was she trying to fool? She had fallen for the guy, and no amount of lying to herself would alter the fact that she had to put a brake on this thing *now*. It was just physical attraction, a chemistry bombshell between opposites, but it was hot and strong and incredibly dangerous—for her at least.

'We must pay him back as soon as we can, Mitch.' She took a deep breath and tried to make her voice less shaky. 'Perhaps when we've done this job we'll be in a position to repay at least half of it.'

'Perhaps,' her brother agreed quietly. 'Although, like I said, he's in no hurry—'

'Well, I am.' Her voice had been too sharp and she moderated it quickly. 'He's done us an enormous favour and I don't want him to think we might take advantage. I'd be the same with anyone,' she added defensively, when Mitch still didn't speak.

'Right.' Mitch cleared his throat and changed the subject. 'How did things go today?'

They discussed the day's events for a few minutes more before finishing the call, but the earlier conversation got between Miriam and the time schedule over and over again in the following hour before bed. When she found herself thinking of several perfectly ridiculous ideas to pay him back she caught her thoughts abruptly, forcing herself to stop.

They hadn't asked him to do this; he had done it quite willingly because, presumably, he'd wanted to, and he was prepared to wait until the debt could be paid. She would make sure that every spare penny went into doing just that and now she had to leave the matter alone, she told herself firmly. She would thank him tomorrow for his help, make sure he understood that repayment was a priority and then let the thing drop. She slid into bed with a determined nod. No problem.

Vera and Dave used their own car for work the next morning, now that they knew where the house was, and left early for an open evening at their son's school. Miriam hadn't seen Reece in the morning but had arrived at the house to find that he had established Mrs Goode downstairs in the drawing room, with a wheelchair within reach if she needed to get about, and had left a note for her from Barbara, who had thought of some last-minute items she wanted adding to the menus.

She worked solidly all day without even stopping for lunch, and was just wiping down the work surfaces in the kitchen, preparatory to leaving, when the same sixth sense as before brought her head turning to the doorway.

'Hi.' He had obviously changed after leaving the office, unless he usually wore jeans and a denim shirt for big business, she thought silently as she nodded her reply to his greeting. And he looked gorgeous. 'Everything going to plan?' he asked lazily as he levered himself off the doorframe where he had been leaning watching her.

'More or less.' She smiled carefully.

'You look tired.' She stared at him in surprise, not knowing quite how to respond as he walked across to stand in front of her, his eyes thoughtful as he lifted her head by tilting her chin gently with one hand and looked down into her face. 'I suppose you just had a sandwich again for lunch?' he asked disapprovingly.

'Lunch?' she asked faintly. 'I didn't have any lunch. An order was delivered just as we were going to eat soup and rolls, and by the time I'd finished checking things in...' Her voice trailed away as the silver eyes took on a distinctly steely hue.

'You didn't bother to eat,' he finished for her. 'Well, you make sure from now on that you take time out at lunchtime; I mean it, Miriam.' He stepped back a pace and surveyed her condemningly, his gaze piercing. 'It won't help anyone if you fall ill, and Barbara's wedding is only days away now.'

The wedding—the damn wedding, she thought tightly. That was the only thing of concern to him in all of this; she might have known. And she had to talk to him about the Gregory matter.

'And stop frowning,' he added drily. 'That's my prerogative.'

'I wanted to talk to you,' she said quickly. 'About the money you paid to the garage. We must put things on a legal footing, Reece—arrange an amount to be repaid each month.'

'Must we?' He crossed his arms in the gesture that was becoming familiar to her and stared down at her with narrowed silver eyes. 'Why?'

'Why?' She waved her hands helplessly. 'Well, it's obvious, isn't it? You can't go around lending people money and saying they can pay you back whenever they like—'

'Oh, I don't.' He smiled slowly. 'Believe me, I don't, Miriam.'

'No, well, then...' She really wasn't handling this very well, she thought weakly. 'You shouldn't with us either.'

'You're friends of Frank,' he said mildly as he settled himself on one of the high breakfast stools scattered about the vast room. 'You aren't "people". And forget about the loan if it troubles you—look on it as a bonus for helping Barbara out.'

No way. She stared at him as though he were mad. 'You're paying us for doing this job and the loan is something quite separate. I've still got to settle up with you for my car too.'

'What *is* this preoccupation with money tonight?' he drawled mockingly as his eyes wandered over her troubled face and wide eyes. 'Do you imagine I shall want something other than financial reimbursement? Is that it?'

'No, that is not it,' she snapped angrily. 'And there is no way on this earth I'd agree to anything like that anyway.'

'Pity.' His smile was a white flash in the dark face and she saw that for once he was genuinely amused. 'If you knew the number of times I'd been propositioned exactly along those lines, and the one time I might consider it it's no go.' His smile widened at her outraged face. 'There's no justice in this world,' he said softly. 'No justice at all.'

'You're just...just—'

'Hungry.' He interrupted her shaking voice firmly as he stood up again, smiling and amused. 'I will go and change into something more formal and then we will go out to dinner.'

'We won't.' It was the most ungracious refusal that she had ever made, although that fact didn't occur to her until much later. Now all she was concerned about was the almost tangible arrogance of the man. 'And I've got my cheque-book with me, so if you will just tell me how much I owe you for the car—'

'How much?' He eyed her quietly as the laughter slid from his face. 'You're determined to consider yourself in debt to me?'

'Yes.' She forced a smile from somewhere, although he would never know the effort it cost. 'It was very kind of you—'

'Don't go all through that again,' he countered irritably. 'Well, if you absolutely insist, the price is going out for dinner with me,' he said grimly, 'although I have to say this is the first time I have had to force a woman to spend an evening in my company.'

'Don't be ridiculous.' Her chin jutted out at an impossible angle and spoke volumes to the man watching her so closely.

'I'm not.' His voice was very cold and very menacing.

'I couldn't possibly go out to dinner dressed like this anyway,' she said quickly as she gestured at the old cotton trousers and casual cotton jumper that she had worn for the day's work. 'I was just going to call in for a hamburger on the way home. I tell you what,' she added slowly as she glanced up into his darkly frowning face, 'I'll treat you to dinner at a hamburger joint as payment for the car, yes?'

'You'll...' She was immensely pleased to notice that he was lost for words and pressed home her advantage quickly.

'Treat *you*, yes. It probably won't be as much as you paid out, but—'

'It'll be fine.' He had clearly decided to concede and shook his head as he gazed down into her smiling face. 'Am I allowed to take you in my car or have I got to endure more hospitality by riding in the rust-bucket?'

'We'll go in your car,' she said cheerfully, disguising her incredulity that he had actually agreed to her impulsive suggestion with enormous will-power. 'And at least you won't have to change now, will you?'

'True.' He shook his head again as he watched her fetch her coat, and held it for her as she slipped her arms in the sleeves. 'We'll go out the front way so I can let Jinny know what's happening. Mrs Goode has already retired for the night; this accident has knocked it out of her more than she will admit. I've been trying to get her to retire for the last couple of years, buy her a little bungalow somewhere, but she won't hear of it.'

He sounded worried and Miriam realised with a little throb of pleasure and surprise that he had actually let his guard down for a few minutes, that he was *really* talking to her about something that mattered to him.

'Well, you told me she's been with you since you were born,' she said carefully as they left the corridor and entered the big hall. 'I suppose it'd be like leaving her family—being turned out, so to speak. Has she got anyone of her own?'

'No.' He shook his head slowly. 'Her husband died before she came to work for my father and they had no children. I think there's a sister somewhere, but they only communicate with Christmas cards to my knowledge.'

'There you are, then.' She shook her head mentally at his lack of perception. 'Don't you see you are all she's got? I noticed the two of you get on very well.'

'Yes.' She had clearly disturbed him with this new angle on things and he said no more as they crossed the hall and entered the main house.

He called Jinny and explained that they were going out to dinner, although she noticed that he didn't explain where and bit back a smile at the knowledge that he was more than a little embarrassed at the circumstances. Then they left the house and walked over to the Bentley parked on the drive, its beautiful pale gold paintwork gleaming silver in the moonlight. The night was crystal-clear and bitingly cold, the smell of frost already cutting the air with its distinctive fragrance.

'You'll have to direct me once we're on the main road,' he said shortly as he opened her door. 'I'm not sure which particular place you mean.'

'OK.' She smiled up at him brightly, suddenly deciding to make the most of an evening that would only ever be a one-off, and he looked down at her for a long moment before shutting the door, his face unreadable.

As they drove into the large car park she had to bite back a wry smile as Reece parked the car between an old, beaten-up Mini and a less than clean breakdown truck. There was every kind of vehicle known to man in the big compound but only one Bentley, and it sat like a king among paupers as they walked over to the brightly lit building and through the main entrance into an atmosphere heavily redolent of beefburgers and French fries.

Reece stopped just inside the door, glancing round the huge room with a distant, aloof expression on his cold face, but Miriam sensed instinctively that the cool, implacable exterior hid a certain degree of uncertainty. He was out of his depth, she realised suddenly with a dart of amazement. In one of the most ordinary places on earth. It was almost as though he had never been in a fast-food establishment before.

'Shall we?' As he gestured towards a vacant table the suspicion became a certainty.

'We go to the far end and order first,' she said quietly as she indicated the long counter behind which several young, uniformed staff were desperately trying to keep up with demand. 'Then wait for the food and take it to a vacant table.'

'Right.' He looked down at her, the silver-grey eyes intent as they swept across her upturned face, his hard-boned features vitally handsome in the harsh lights overhead. 'Then lead on Macduff; I'm all yours.'

She was unprepared for the fierce stab of pain that hit her in her heart region at his casual words, and it could have been a nasty moment, but even as he spoke he had ushered her forward in front of him so her face was hidden from view. Sexual interest, animal chemistry, she told herself violently as they walked down the narrow aisle. It means nothing, *nothing* in the wider scope of things, don't forget it.

And by the look of things she wasn't the only one affected either.

'Yes?' The attractive redhead behind the counter ignored several people in front of them and spoke directly to Reece over Miriam's head. 'What can I get for you?' she asked cheekily, with the sort of wide-eyed smile that was an anomaly in the frantic tempo of the place.

'The lady's calling the tune.' She just knew that Reece was smiling at the girl from the note in his voice and would have loved to kick him hard. 'This is her treat,' he added smoothly.

'Lucky you.' As the girl grinned at her Miriam made an effort and smiled back. 'Now, what do you want?'

A few minutes later they were seated at a table with a mountain of food between them. 'Are you really going to eat all that?' Miriam asked in amazement as Reece bit into the first of the quarter-pounders he had ordered complete with French fries and all the trimmings.

'It's very good.' His grin made her breath catch in her throat and set the warning bell jangling madly. 'I get the distinct feeling I've been missing out all these years.'

'You haven't been here before?' she asked carefully, relaxing as one black eyebrow raised sardonically at her tact.

'That wasn't too hard to work out, was it?' He shrugged slowly. 'Barbara and I were brought up with enormous wealth, Miriam, but the normal things...' He shook his head quietly. 'I guess they just didn't happen for us. We had an excellent education—I'm not complaining—and I think my first meal out was at the Ritz when I was still in a high chair.'

He smiled, his eyes distant, and she forced herself to show none of the sympathy his words had aroused, knowing that it would be offensive to him. 'From when I was knee-high we were indoctrinated to take care of ourselves, show no emotion and conduct ourselves in a manner befitting the Vance name. Appearances were everything to my parents, and to the set in which they moved.'

'And you?' She looked at him hard as he bit into the beefburger. 'Where did that leave you?'

'Realistic,' he said coldly. 'The world is motivated by power and influence, Miriam, and don't let anyone persuade you otherwise. Poets and philosophers may expound on the goodly virtues but they don't stand the test in the market-place where it's still dog eat dog.'

'But—' She stopped abruptly at the flinty hardness in his face. 'You don't mean that,' she said weakly. 'Surely you aren't saying that honesty and integrity are wrong?'

'No, I'm not saying they are wrong,' he responded quietly, his voice cool and contained. 'Personally I live by my own moral code, which includes honesty and integrity, but I *am* saying that I walk this road with my eyes wide open. I can be as ruthless as the next man, more so if necessary, and especially when I am crossed. I don't expect any favours from anyone and I don't ask for any. In the final analysis everyone is looking out for themselves first, second and third. I have no illusions.'

'I don't believe that.' She stared at him indignantly, quite forgetting to eat herself as he finished his first beefburger and began on the second with every appearance of enjoyment. 'About everyone looking out for themselves first. Where does love feature in this world of yours if that's the case?'

'Love?' He leant back in his chair as he eyed her mockingly, his eyes cool slits of silver in an otherwise expressionless face. 'Love is the original four-letter word that has been so misused through the ages that I'm amazed it isn't regarded as obscene. Even the dictionary definition is ambiguous, covering more doubtful emotions than you've had hot dinners in the last month.' He raised his eyebrows sardonically. 'Warm affection is one, and benevolence, charity, to admire passionately, sexual passion...' He paused and nodded slowly. 'Now that last one is perhaps the nearest to anything honest, although another definition, a score of nothing, has merit.'

'That means in tennis,' she said hotly as his cynicism hit a raw nerve. 'And love isn't sexual passion—well, not altogether,' she corrected herself quickly. 'It's lots of things for different kinds of love; surely you can accept that? The love a man and woman feel is different to the one of a mother for her baby—'

'In my case it was extremely different,' he said drily as he gestured for her to eat. 'Barbara and I saw our parents for ten minutes in the evening, if we were lucky, from the day we were born until we left for boarding-school at the age of seven. The rest of the time we were in the care of people who were paid to look after us. Some did their job well and others weren't so conscientious, but nevertheless it was still just a job.

'I'm sorry, Miriam, but I don't believe in this rose-coloured fantasy called love, not in any form. I simply don't believe it exists beyond the desire to believe in the concept by weak-willed individuals who don't have what it takes to get through by themselves.'

'That's awful.' She stared at him aghast, her eyes huge in her distress as she forgot all about herself in the aftermath of what he had revealed. 'I love lots of people, and not just because I need them to get by,' she added quickly.

'Who?' He leant forward suddenly, his eyes narrowing. 'Who exactly do you love, Miriam?'

'Who?' She bit into her quarter-pounder and chewed stolidly for a minute before swallowing, to give herself time to think. These revelations had hit her far harder than she would have liked; in fact the place where her stomach should have been was a churning mass of jelly. But only because she felt sorry for him, she told herself quickly as she swallowed the food past the huge lump in her throat and took a quick gulp of cola. That was all. 'Well, there's my mother for a start, and Mitch, and my grandparents who live in Scotland—'

'They are all people you have been programmed to consider you love since you were a child,' he interrupted coldly. 'As I'm a child of my heritage, so are you.'

'And friends.' She eyed him firmly, a small shred of anger beginning to burn deep inside at his apparent scepticism. 'I've several dear friends, one or two that I've known since childhood, who I love, although I suppose I've never put it into words before.'

'And boyfriends?' He leant back again and took a long swallow of his drink. 'Have you *loved* a boy before?'

'I'm not sure how you mean that.' She glared at him as the anger began to flare more strongly. 'And you needn't put that scornful emphasis on the word "love" either. I now what I feel, Reece, and neither you nor all the powers in the universe could make me say any different. There are people that I care about more than myself; I love them, and that's that.'

She eyed him defiantly as her cheeks glowed scarlet. 'I don't care whether you say love exists or not—I know it does; I've felt it and it's got nothing to do with how much money someone's got or how influential they are either. I think your outlook on life stinks,' she finished tightly as she rammed what was left of the unfortunate bun into her mouth and chewed ferociously.

'Everyone to their own, Miriam.' He was as cool and remote as ever, his face unreadable, and for a moment the urge to hit him was as strong as the urge to reach across and kiss him, and the latter frightened her far more than the former.

Somehow the revelations about his boyhood had pierced something deep inside and it was hurting still more with every second that ticked by. It was ridiculous, crazy, but she had never felt the urge to comfort someone as strongly as she was feeling it now, and the urge was *very* physical and definitely quite carnal, she reflected painfully.

She wished that they hadn't taken the job, wished that she hadn't come here with him tonight; in fact she wished that she'd never laid eyes on Reece Vance. No, she didn't. She glanced at him as the last of his meal disappeared and then looked down at her cold French fries. No, she didn't, and that in itself was the craziest thing of all.

'I've upset you.' She kept her eyes on the table and then jumped violently as his hand closed over hers. 'I've upset you, haven't I?' he asked softly, in a voice that would have melted solid stone.

'Don't be silly.' She dodged the question as she carefully extracted her hand from under his. 'You're entitled to your opinion, after all.'

'Even if it stinks?' he asked wryly.

'Even then.' It cost her more than he would ever know to raise her head and smile, but she did just that even as her heart began to pound frantically at the rueful, tender expression on his face. He looked almost as though he cared that he'd hurt her, she thought agonisingly, watching the silver eyes darken as they wandered over her half-open mouth, but of course he didn't. Reece Vance wouldn't countenance such an emotion.

'Honesty has its price.' He shrugged as he withdrew his hand and finished the last of his drink. 'I could have given you a line but that wouldn't have been fair, and most women—'

He stopped abruptly and she tensed inside, sensing that she wouldn't like what he was about to say but unable to leave it alone anyway. 'Most women?' she asked softly.

'Most women are quite happy to take the good times along with all the material benefits of a relationship and leave it at that,' he said quietly.

'I think you've been mixing with the wrong women.' His eyes shot to her face as she spoke but she stared back at him bravely as she forced herself to say what she thought. 'In fact I'd hardly call such people women at all. All the ones I know value friendship and a degree of commitment in a relationship far more than what they can get out of it materially. Not all of them are seeking the love a lifetime, no. I can think of one or two of my friends who have been with their partners for some time because they simply enjoy their company and respect the people they are, but love often starts like that anyway. It isn't always an instant blinding light, whatever the poets might say.'

'And you're an authority on the subject?' he asked coolly, but with a cutting edge to his voice that told her the indulgence he had displayed so far had vanished.

'I don't have to be to give my point of view,' she answered crisply.

'True...' He gave her a long, sardonic glance and then changed the subject abruptly as he gestured at his empty tray. 'I really enjoyed that,' he said politely, but with a shred of surprise in his deep voice that told her the comment was genuine. 'It's probably murder on the digestive system but I can see why the kids go for it now.'

He glanced around the room full of a wide assortment of the human race, including truck drivers, families out for an evening snack, young couples and a host of giggling schoolgirls in one corner who were clearly having a birthday treat. 'And the oldies too.'

'How the other half live?' she suggested drily, and as his gaze snapped back to her she saw the silver eyes were narrowed and watchful. 'Perhaps they don't have such a bad life anyway, even if they aren't setting the world ablaze.' It was probably below the belt, she admitted, even as the words left her lips, but his comments on other women had hit a nerve that wouldn't be calmed.

'I never thought they did.' There was no laughter or amusement in his voice now, nor the overt, laconic mockery with which she had expected him to meet her taunt, but as his eyes met hers for the briefest of moments she saw a passionate, hungry desire in the silver-grey depths that robbed her of speech and froze her thought processes.

It was instantly veiled as he moved his head to glance casually round the room again, but the brief baring of his soul had shocked her beyond measure. There had been untold hurt in that one piercing glance—hurt and pain and a craving for something that was voracious in its intensity. His lost childhood, perhaps?

She sat still and stunned in her seat as she slowly forced her hand to reach out and raise a stone-cold French fry to her mouth in some semblance of normality.

Or was it something in the present that made him look like that? One thing was for sure—what he said and what he felt were two totally different things with this man. The hard outer shell that he had built round himself was inches thick and it would take some sort of miracle to pierce such armour. Or some woman. Sharon's image floated in her mind's eye in all its exquisite beauty and she felt a cold shiver flicker down her spine. And the beautiful blonde was certainly some woman...

'Did you have a nice time on Saturday?' The second the words had left her lips she would have given the world to take them back, but all she could do was present a smilingly bland face to him as his gaze returned to her.

'Saturday?' His brow wrinkled for a moment and then cleared. 'Oh, Saturday. Well, the meal was excellent—but then the Berkely-Smiths have a reputation for their lavish hospitality which is second to none and must be maintained at all times.' The cynicism was hard and raw. 'It was more of a business evening anyway; Charles and I had several important matters to discuss.'

'Oh, I see.' She knew that she ought to leave it right there, but she also knew that she wasn't going to. 'I thought it was a dinner party?'

'It was,' he said briefly.

'I suppose Sharon's parents like having you around,' she continued carefully. 'You being an old friend of the family and so on.' Mention her. Say *something*, she screamed at him silently. The very fact that he had avoided saying Sharon's name spoke volumes—didn't it?

'Not particularly.' The silver gaze fixed on her face and she forced her eyes to show no reaction. 'I get on quite well with Charles, but Margaret is too like my mother for there to be any rapport between us, and she is astute enough to know I don't like her.'

'You don't like her?' she echoed faintly. 'But you just said she was like your mother—'

'My mother was a cold, predatory, rapacious woman completely devoid of normal human warmth,' Reece said coolly with absolutely no emotion whatsoever. 'Rather as you view me, I suspect,' he added, in a voice that was deceptively casual. 'For some reason I have never been able to fathom, my father adored her, and her slightest wish was his command. She was exceptionally beautiful but he came into contact with many beautiful women. However...' he shrugged slowly '...obviously my mother had something the others hadn't.'

'But she was your *mother*,' Miriam protested faintly. 'You must have felt something for her—'

'You were brought up in a happy, normal home,' Reece said quietly. 'You wouldn't understand.' It hurt—it hurt so much that her skin prickled with cold and her throat felt as rough as sandpaper. What could she say? How could she begin to get through to him when he had just told her that she didn't have a clue what he was talking about?

As the chatter and laughter ebbed and flowed around them she stared at him, searching her mind for a comment that wouldn't seem inane as her heart thudded painfully. She knew somehow that he hadn't talked to anyone like this for a long time; it was there in the hard, straight line of his mouth and the visible withdrawal in his body and face as he glanced round the crowded restaurant. But they were worlds apart. In every way. The knowledge caused her chest to tighten and burn and she felt a physical pain that caught the breath in her throat. She had to say something. She just had to say *something*; she'd probably never get the chance to reach out to him again.

'Anyway, all that was a long time ago and, like the line from the film, "I don't give a damn".' He smiled as his gaze returned to her troubled face, his eyes glittering with a savage self-mockery that belied his words.

'I'm in control of my own life now and I live exactly the way I want to,' he said flatly. 'No false emotion, no promises that are impossible to keep and no ties.'

'And Barbara was the same until now,' she whispered, with a sudden surge of understanding. That was why he couldn't believe his sister's love for her fiancé was genuine. They were twins, each with a twin's capacity for understanding the other's mind, and after the childhood they had had Reece couldn't visualise Barbara taking such a step of faith with another human being. Because he couldn't. Her heart stopped and then thudded on.

'Dead right.' He had heard her whisper and his voice was scathing. 'I don't know what she's playing at but she'd make the worst mother in the world; we've both got some of our mother's blood running through our veins, after all.'

'She loves him, Reece,' Miriam said bleakly. 'She told me so and I believe her.'

'She's a Vance,' Reece said bitterly as his eyes turned into pinpoints of steel. 'She's incapable of love.'

CHAPTER SIX

THEY drove back to the house in virtual silence under a cold, clear sky in which each tiny star was picked out in glittering detail, and Miriam couldn't remember when she had felt more miserable in the whole of her life.

But why? she asked herself angrily a hundred times during the short journey. Reece Vance is nothing to you; his views on women and love are sad but you hardly know the man, for crying out loud. *It doesn't matter.*

But it did, and by the time they reached the long, curving drive leading up to the house her nerves were as taut as piano-wire. She should have said something—anything—instead of sitting there staring at him like a small, dumb sheep, she told herself tightly as he brought the car to a halt just past the house. But she'd blown it; she'd absolutely blown it.

'Miriam.' As he cut the ignition and the powerful engine fell silent Reece turned to her in the soft darkness, one arm sliding round the back of her seat. 'I shouldn't have said all that about Barbara back there. Believe what you want to if it makes you happy; you might be right after all.' There was no chance in the world that he believed that, she thought bleakly as she looked into the hard male face watching her so intently. 'I hardly know Craig—'

'Reece, you're wrong—about anyone being incapable of love,' she said quickly before she lost her nerve. 'Even the worst monsters in history loved someone.'

'Did they?' His voice held that note which she had heard once or twice before—a thick, husky silkiness that melted her bones. 'So fierce and determined, so vulnerable . . .' And then he had taken her mouth in a kiss that made her shake with the sweetness of it, his lips moving coaxingly over hers as he pulled her close to him but with a gentleness that made her feel like something rare and precious in his embrace.

This was a line, just a well-practised line, she told herself helplessly as the kiss became more intimate, his mouth parting her lips with a soft sigh, but it was no good. The blood was pounding through her veins like fire and her ears were singing with a strange heat that took away all coherent thought. He wanted her—physically he wanted her very much, she told herself as the hardness in the big male body so close to hers became apparent. But that was all it was. An animal desire with no commitment, no real tenderness, no future.

But then, as his warm mouth stroked her neck and throat with a hundred fleeting kisses, she ceased to think and just let her senses feel.

His mouth moved back to hers and she realised that he had somehow slipped her coat off her shoulders, moving her slightly so that it fell beneath her waist as his hands moved up under the thin cotton of her jumper and touched the silky skin beneath. His touch was like a million volts of electricity passing right through her and she stiffened with the force of it, but then his hands began a slow, erotic massage over her soft, supple skin and the last of her defences crumbled.

She could feel her body changing to answer the call of his manhood, her softness moist and warm, and knew even in her innocence that she was issuing an invitation that was as old as time and one that his experience wouldn't miss, but it was too late for caution. All she was conscious of were the sensations that his love-making was drawing from her quivering body, and she didn't want them to end—ever.

'Miriam?' His voice was thick and warm against her cheek as he drew back slightly to look at her with narrowed silver eyes. 'Come in for a nightcap? In the warm.' She knew what he was asking but her head nodded anyway, her mouth making a little lost sound as the warmth of his body left hers for a brief moment before he moved round the car to open her door and pull her into his arms again, his mouth hungry and almost savage now as his fierce need took over.

She wanted him—she wanted him so badly that she couldn't believe what she was feeling, but as he moved her into him and turned to walk towards the house a harsh flare of lights blinded her for a moment, causing her head to turn into the wall of his chest.

'What the hell...?' She heard his mutter a second before tyres screeched to a halt just in front of them, and as the lights were dimmed she opened her eyes to confront a sleek red sports car and the blood turned to ice in her veins.

'Darling...' Sharon slid elegantly out of the car, her slim, stockinged legs exquisite in black silk and her silver-blonde hair loose and flowing round her slender shoulders. 'I just had to see you...' Her gaze moved slowly to Miriam, as though she had just noticed her in the crook of Reece's arm. 'Oh, dear.' She smiled slowly. 'Have I come at a bad time, sweetie?'

'Not at all.' Miriam had jerked herself free of Reece's arm before the other woman had finished speaking, her cheeks burning but her eyes wide and clear as they met the hard green gaze head-on. 'I was just leaving; my car's parked round the back.'

'Miriam?' As she turned to make what she had hoped would be a dignified exit Reece caught hold of her arm, totally ignoring Sharon. 'I thought you were coming in for coffee?'

'Some other time.' She forced the hurt and anger that she was feeling inside to the back of her mind as she gave him a brittle, bright smile and carefully extracted her arm from his hold. 'I've masses to do tomorrow and some paperwork to finish tonight before I call it a day.'

'Please don't leave on my account,' Sharon drawled sweetly as she drew her long, expensive coat round her slim shape before slamming the driver's door shut. 'Reece is used to my dropping by whenever the need takes me, aren't you, sweetie?' She raised brilliant green eyes to Reece's face and then froze for a second before glancing hastily at Miriam again.

'I'm leaving because I have work to do,' Miriam said expressionlessly, knowing that she had to get away before she said something she'd regret for the rest of her life. 'Goodnight.' She turned to Reece and saw that his face was stony-hard, the silver-grey eyes lethal. 'Goodnight,' she said again breathlessly as she ducked her head and began walking, fast.

She heard his deep, cold voice say something to Sharon but couldn't make out the words through the pounding in her ears, and then, mercifully, she was round the side of the house and scurrying like a small rabbit to its hole as she neared her car.

'Start, please start; tonight of all nights, start,' she begged the cold engine frantically as she turned the ignition, hearing the cough and sneeze as it spluttered into life with a feeling of deep gratitude.

She went through the motions of reversing the car automatically, her mind buzzing with a thousand screaming recriminations, and then roared off down the drive far too quickly towards the main road, executing what virtually constituted an emergency stop before turning onto the main highway with her palms damp and her face wet.

She was a fool, such a fool, she told herself fiercely as the little car skidded through the traffic. To allow him such liberties when he had just told her that any sort of emotional commitment was anathema to him. She wiped the hot tears off her face with the back of her hand and ground her teeth loudly in the darkness. *Fool, fool, fool.*

She shook her head and then heard the blaring of a horn just behind her and realised that she had veered halfway across the outside lane. She'd have to pull over; she wasn't safe to drive like this. She managed to get off the dual carriageway at the next turn-off and drove along a quiet residential street before turning into an empty bus pull-in and switching off the ignition with shaking fingers.

The urge to cry had gone now, to be replaced with a stunned, icy-cold desperation that chilled her very bones. She *was* a fool, the biggest one ever born, she realised, because she suddenly understood the reason for her total weakness where Reece Vance was concerned. It wasn't just physical attraction, a chemistry explosion of the senses, although those things were very real. She loved him.

She groaned out loud and hit her fist against the inoffensive steering wheel. How it had happened, when, she wasn't quite sure but it was a fact. She loved a man who didn't even understand the meaning of the word and, what was more, had a host of women, one of whom he was with now, who could outshine her in every way.

How long she sat there she didn't know, but when, after a long, long time, she started the car again her mind was calm if painfully savaged. She loved him. She was achingly sorry for all the hurt and pain he had suffered in the past, but one thing was crystal-clear. She had to protect herself, raise a barrier between Reece Vance and herself that was impenetrable, because he had the power to destroy her—to rip her to shreds and then walk away without even knowing he had done so. Perhaps Sharon and the others could take the terms he offered and be satisfied with physical gratification and material gain but she couldn't.

She pictured his big, lean body and hard-planed male face and felt a sense of loss that was indescribable. Was it possible to mourn what you'd never had? She nodded to herself bitterly. Too true.

She didn't sleep at all that night, and when morning sent the first pink rays of a new day over the horizon she forced herself to shower and dress, eating breakfast mechanically as she watched the sky change from pink-streaked grey to light-washed blue.

She didn't want to see him ever again and yet she did, desperately. Was it possible to fall in love with someone so hard so quickly? She shook her head at her own stupidity. Why was she asking herself that question when she knew the answer only too well? And Reece thought love was an illusion. Her mouth straightened into a tight line of pain as she felt the sickening lurch in her stomach that accompanied such thoughts. If only, oh, if only...

She arrived at the Vance residence a few minutes before nine. She could have started work an hour or two earlier—it would have been preferable to sitting at home with her thoughts—but Reece might have thought that she had arrived early in order to have some time alone with him and she couldn't have coped with that eventuality.

Vera and Dave were already hard at work preparing the ingredients for their famous pâté when she arrived, and after checking the schedule for the day she walked gingerly through the hall into the main house to confer with Mrs Goode. She was anxious that the elderly housekeeper felt included in all the preparations for Barbara's wedding; from what Reece had told her the night before, Mrs Goode was as much a part of the family as any blood relative.

She found the little woman in the drawing room in front of a roaring log fire, and as she peered carefully round the door the housekeeper glanced up from the book she was reading and smiled instantly.

'Miriam. Do come and sit down a moment, dear.'

'I was looking for you, Mrs Goode,' Miriam said quietly as she sank down next to the frail little figure and smiled warmly. 'There are a couple of things I wanted to ask your opinion about.'

'You're a good girl, Miriam.' The remark took Miriam by surprise and she stared at the older woman for a moment in consternation. 'I can see that you can handle this perfectly well without an old woman messing things up,' Mrs Goode continued perkily, 'but that's not your way, is it? "Bonny and blithe and good and gay..."'

'He didn't tell you about the rhyme?' Miriam asked as hot colour flooded the pale silk of her skin.

'Only in the most complimentary way,' Mrs Goode answered quickly. 'He...admires you very much, Miriam; you must know that.'

'You think so?' Miriam smiled flatly. Admired? And what sort of emotion did he feel for the lovely Sharon? 'Well, that's good, especially if he puts it down on paper when the job is finished. Most of our contracts are by word of mouth in this business.'

'Yes...' Mrs Goode seemed about to say more, but Miriam continued quickly before she could speak.

'Now, I was wondering about the seating arrangements for the buffet? Perhaps you could suggest...?'

The next few minutes were spent discussing technicalities, and as she rose to leave Miriam forced herself to speak the name that had been hovering on her lips all morning. 'Did Reece tell you about the decision on the flowers, Mrs Goode? Barbara wanted no silk, only fresh ones, so I've arranged for a little firm we deal with to come in on the day and fix them. I think we'll have enough to do without worrying about the flowers.' She smiled warmly.

'No, he didn't mention it, dear.' Mrs Goode shook her head. 'But then he was in a bit of a tizzy when he spoke to me last night.'

'Was he?' Her heart thudded to a standstill and then raced on at a furious pace that made her feel quite dizzy. 'Why was that?' she asked carefully.

'Oh, some problem on an overseas contract he's involved with.' Mrs Goode sniffed disapprovingly. 'Rang him here at home at ten o'clock last night, so they did. Got no respect for people's privacy, have they? Anyway, he called by my room to say he'd got to catch the six o'clock flight to France, so I suppose everything else went from his mind.'

'Yes, I suppose it did,' she agreed mechanically as she berated herself fiercely for the surge of hope that the housekeeper's words had given her. He had probably forgotten that she existed the moment the call had come through—or some time before that if Sharon had stayed. She thought again about the black-stockinged legs and classic little black dress that she had glimpsed fleetingly before Sharon had pulled her coat tight around her. And she would have stayed. She hadn't dressed like that for an evening at home in front of the TV.

And to think that she had been willing to give herself to Reece last night! She bit down on her lower lip hard. Willing? She had all but begged him to take her, she thought miserably as she remembered her uninhibited responses to his lovemaking.

'Are you all right, dear?' She came back to the present to find Mrs Goode staring up at her with a worried expression adding more lines to the paper-thin skin. 'You look a little peaky.'

'I'm fine.' Or I intend to be, she added to herself firmly as she walked out of the room a moment or two later. There was no way she was going to crumple like a piece of discarded paper over this. She *wouldn't*. Her eyes darkened with resolve. She was a big girl now, partner in a successful catering firm, with her own career mapped out and the world her oyster. Reece Vance wasn't the only man in the world by a long chalk. But even as she thought them the words rang hollow and empty in the depths of her mind, mockingly unreal.

The next few days raced by in a whirl of activity that left no room for morbid post-mortems, and Miriam embraced the frantic schedule gratefully. She arrived home too tired to think, often slipping into bed without bothering to eat and falling asleep as soon as her head touched the pillow.

Reece apparently phoned every day to check progress with Mrs Goode, and she made sure that she gave the housekeeper a report on the day's happenings each night before she left to avoid any necessity of speaking to Reece personally.

She could get through like this—she *could*, she told herself firmly on the fourth day of Reece's absence; it wasn't so hard really. Once he was out of her life for good it would be easy to pick up the threads again and carry on as though nothing had happened. The sick feeling in her stomach, the blanking of her mind at every opportunity, the weird dreams at night and frantic pounding of her heart in the day—all perfectly copeable with. And the urge to cry at the oddest times, the desolate pain—she'd master those too.

She was still persuading herself that everything was under control on the Wednesday before the wedding, after a particularly chaotic day when everything that could have gone wrong had done so. It was seven o'clock at night, she hadn't even begun to clear away the debris of the day and already she was a few hours behind her tight schedule that didn't allow any leeway. Two days to go. She shut her eyes and prayed for calm. They'd do it— they had to do it. But right now she was too tired to think straight.

'You look terrible.' She froze for just an instant before looking towards the door at the large male figure standing silently just inside the room. He looked tired, and utterly gorgeous. That much registered before she wrenched her eyes away and grabbed a large bin-bag of rubbish that she intended to take to the dustbins outside.

'Thank you so much,' she said sarcastically as she whisked a few more items of litter off the worktops into the bag. He'd been away a week and that was all he could manage? She hadn't expected any bouquets, but she was blowed if she was going to put up with this. 'You don't look so hot yourself,' she added tartly as an empty tin did a hop, skip and a jump off the worktop, scattering the last few drips of raspberry sauce all over her pale blue trousers.

Damn, damn, damn! She pushed back her mane of silky red hair that had long ago discarded its ribbon to lie in a flame-coloured sheen around her shoulders and prayed that the tears of exhaustion and rage wouldn't show in her voice. She hated him—she really hated him.

'I didn't mean you look terrible.' He had moved behind her to swing her round so quickly that she had no chance to escape his hold. 'Just...terrible.' He kissed the tip of her nose with great seriousness. 'Tired, exhausted, worn out.' He kissed her again. 'But still the best thing on two legs I've seen for a long time.'

'You obviously haven't been looking properly,' she said weakly, trying to summon up more anger to replace the rage that had melted the minute he had touched her.

How could he come back after being away so long and expect her to fall into his arms the moment he raised his little finger? But then... Her innate honesty came uncomfortably to the fore. She had done exactly that a few nights ago, and just after he had expressly laid out the guidelines for anyone foolish enough to get involved with him. Of course he had gone away thinking that she was his for the taking, easy, available, she berated herself bitterly. What else was there for him to think?

'I've missed you.' There was that note of surprise in his voice again, but she was too distressed to hear it. 'And thought about you a lot.'

'Have you?' She took a deep breath. 'Reece, there's something I have to explain to you—'

'This hair—this wonderfully alive hair...' He brushed his open fingers along the side of her cheeks and fanned her hair out into a red cloud. 'I've never seen anything like it in my life. You're beautiful, Miriam.' As he bent to take her lips she retained enough sense to lower her head quickly, moving out of his arms in one swift movement as she nerved herself for what she had to say.

She had to make him understand that she couldn't have a casual affair, become his plaything for a few weeks or perhaps months, until he tired of her.

She brushed her hair back behind her ears and turned to face him, wishing desperately that she had worn something other than an old T-shirt and somewhat worn trousers. But she hadn't known that he was coming home tonight, no one had said, and, anyway, maybe it was better that he saw her like this. He'd already said that she looked terrible, after all.

'Reece, that other night.' She looked full into his face for the first time, and the knowledge of his power over her hit her afresh as she watched the beautiful silver-grey eyes narrow with sudden watchfulness.

'Yes?' He made no attempt to touch her now, moving back a pace and crossing his arms as he looked down at her from a face that could have been carved in stone.

'I wouldn't like you to get the wrong impression,' she murmured weakly. 'I don't—' She stopped abruptly and then forced herself to continue. 'I don't sleep around, however it might have seemed—'

'It *seemed* as though we shared a few kisses,' Reece said softly. 'How did it seem to you?'

'You know what I mean.' How could she want to run and fling herself into his arms, she asked herself incredulously, after all that he had said that night? But she did. Achingly so. The traitorous weakness made her voice even stronger when next she spoke. 'And it was more than just a few kisses anyway. You were very explicit about how you view women, Reece—I had no excuse—but I'm not into casual affairs.' Unlike Sharon, she added silently.

'You want me, Miriam,' he said expressionlessly. 'You might not want to hear that but we both know it's the truth. Maybe you don't even like me, but your body knows exactly what it wants. And I know you aren't into affairs, casual or otherwise, but surely you don't intend to remain chaste for the rest of your life?'

'What I do or don't intend is nothing to do with you, Reece.' She had to be strong now, she told herself as a fierce pain at his apparently unemotional stating of the facts pierced her through. 'You were frank with me and now I'm being frank with you. I don't like the way you live, the way those women live. I couldn't be like that, and what's more I don't want to be. I find it...unacceptable and distasteful.'

'I wouldn't have thought you were the sort of person to sit in judgement of others so harshly,' he said coolly, still in that remote, cold voice that had no warmth or emotion in its depths.

'Neither would I,' she answered honestly, 'so it looks like I've surprised both of us.' Can't you see how much I love you? she asked him silently as she made her face as blank as his. Can't you see why the thought of you in another woman's arms makes me feel sick to my bones? How can you want Sharon and me at the same time?

'You know I'm attracted to you?' he asked flatly.

'Physically? Yes.' She nodded. 'As you've just said so succinctly we seem to strike some sort of spark off each other, but I'm sure that isn't a first with you.' She eyed him calmly as her heart pounded so hard that she was sure he could hear it. 'You think there's nothing wrong in wanting someone and fulfilling that need—'

'Hang on a minute,' he said roughly as his eyes darkened ominously. 'I don't know what that imagination of yours has been brewing but I don't go in for casual sex, if that's what you're insinuating. I won't deny I've been involved with a few women in my time, but at thirty-five you'd hardly expect to find me having lived the life of a monk, would you? I'm a normal man, Miriam, and a life of chastity is only for the very noble or those minus the baser urges, and I make no apology for fitting into neither category. That doesn't mean I've been running around like some sort of deranged debauchee since puberty. Each relationship I've had has meant something and lasted some time—'

'But you've never loved them,' she said tightly as a mixture of painful jealousy and sudden anger at his remoteness had her fighting to stay calm.

'No.' He was quite still, watching her. 'Would it have been better if I'd pretended I had? If I'd lied to you?'

'And you wouldn't love me,' she continued, as though he hadn't spoken. 'You've made that perfectly clear.'

'Does that matter?' he asked softly. 'You've also made it perfectly clear that I'm not exactly your ideal man. Couldn't we just take it a day at a time and see how we get to know each other?'

'In bed,' she said flatly. Not her ideal man? This had to be the ultimate irony.

'Not necessarily.' He smiled slowly. 'I can think of other places if you'd prefer.'

'I don't.' She didn't respond to his attempt to lighten the situation by so much as the flicker of an eyelash. 'You just don't see, do you, Reece? You're trying to seduce me at the same time as warning me that I'll never mean anything to you. You might call that being honest but I call it being cowardly.'

His face straightened now, his skin flushing a deep dark red as his eyes glittered hotly.

'You'll probably laugh your head off at this, but when I give myself to a man I want to at least be able to hope it will last for ever, be able to see myself with him for more than a few weeks or months. And *I* make no apology for that!' She took a deep breath and lowered her voice, which had begun to rise. 'I want my partner to think I'm the most precious thing on this earth, that there is no one like me,' she continued more quietly. 'I want a home and children and—'

'Slippers by the fire?' he asked with cutting coldness.

'Exactly.' She faced him without flinching at the mockery. 'Just that. I don't want to have to wonder who the next lady in his life will be, to watch each new face that comes on his horizon and wonder if this will be the one who replaces me.'

'Dammit, it wouldn't be like that,' he ground out through clenched teeth, his eyes furious. 'You're making it sound as though all the odds are loaded on my side—'

'They would be.' She prayed that she could say what she had to say without giving herself away. 'With someone like me they would be. Perhaps not the other women that you've had affairs with—you'd be the best judge of that—but with me it wouldn't be the same. I couldn't give myself to you without loving you,' she added quietly, knowing that it was the one thing that would send him away. 'And we both know that that is impossible.' Because you wouldn't allow yourself to love me back, she added silently as his face whitened. 'Even if you wanted to, which you don't.'

'Impossible. Yes, I see.' The withdrawal in his face and body was a physical thing although he didn't move an inch. 'Then I think we've taken this discussion as far as it can go,' he said coldly. 'Thank you for your frankness.'

She had to force the flood of love and passion and tenderness that rushed in unawares at the sight of his white, still face back into the deep recesses of her mind as he turned and walked over to the doorway. She was angry with him for hurting her like this, furious that he wasn't even prepared to try and understand how she felt, but overall the main emotion was one of terrible sadness at the inevitability of it all. She hated him and loved him all in the same breath, and the hopelessness of it all was too painful to bear.

'I gather by the state of this kitchen and your general air of weariness that things haven't gone too well,' he said frostily as he turned and surveyed her from the doorway with chillingly neutral eyes.

'No, everything's fine, but today we got a bit behind,' she answered mechanically as she lowered her head and

busied herself wiping the big work surfaces as she spoke.
'I shall stay here an hour or so more and catch up, and
then—'

'The temporary staff are arriving tomorrow?' he interrupted flatly.

'Yes.' She bit back the urge to fly at him for his
rudeness. 'Mrs Goode is going to oversee them and explain everything that is needed. I understand Craig's relations are coming to stay on Friday?' He nodded
without speaking as she darted a glance at him. 'Mrs
Goode and Jinny have prepared the guest rooms, so
everything is under control.'

'Hardly.' The hard gaze flickered round the chaos in
the kitchen. 'I would suggest you bring a case with you
tomorrow and plan on being here for the next three or
four days. You did assure me at the time of accepting
the job that that would be no problem,' he added icily
as she began to shake her head at the suggestion.

'But...' Her voice faltered as she glanced round the
room. There was nothing else for it; she would have to
move into the flat for a couple of days. That way she
would be right on hand for any emergencies that might
arise, and at the very least it would give her another two
or three hours of working time a day. And she needed
every minute.

'Fine,' she agreed stiffly. 'Mitch and the others have
been working here through the day since Monday, and
in spite of how things may appear tonight I can assure
you there are no problems.'

'Good.' There was no vestige of the ardent lover in
the shuttered face that looked at her so coldly. 'Keep it
that way, please.' And then he was gone and she leant
shakily against the edge of the cupboards as her legs
turned liquid.

The swine—the cold-blooded, callous swine... She
found her mind listing a number of expletives as she
struggled for composure. How dared he come back and
proposition her like that anyway—she shook her head

blindly as she fought back acid tears—and then virtually accuse her of not doing her job properly when she didn't fall into his arms? She loathed him—she *did*.

The fury began to take over and quell the trembling, bringing her bolt upright as she vented her wrath on the hapless kitchen, clearing up in half the time it normally took her. And to think that she had thought she loved him! She must have been crazy—

'Miriam?' Barbara's dark head appeared round the door a second after her knock. 'Reece said you might still be here. I'm glad we haven't missed you. I wanted you to meet Craig.'

'Barbara.' She had quite forgotten that Reece's sister and her fiancé were due to arrive that evening, but now, as a massive giant of a man followed Barbara into the room, she just caught a glimpse of Reece scowling darkly in the doorway before her gaze switched to Craig's smiling face.

'Hiya...' She found herself enfolded in a pair of giant arms that would have done credit to any Mr Universe and felt her ribs creak in protest. 'I understand we have a lot to thank you for, Miriam,' Barbara's fiancé said cheerfully as he moved back a pace and surveyed her with a pair of the bluest eyes she had ever seen. 'It can't have been easy to take over like this.'

'It's what she gets paid for.' Reece's voice was liquid ice as he moved to their side, and his grey eyes were splintered points of light in his dark face as he glared at Craig.

'Well, yeh...' Craig was clearly out of his depth, and Miriam couldn't blame him. She had never seen such coldness in another human being's face, and all the poor man had done was thank her for helping them out with the wedding. She glared at Reece in her turn, quite forgetting Craig and Barbara for a moment, and they looked on with mounting interest at the little scene being enacted in front of them.

'Nevertheless, it is nice to know *someone* round here appreciates all the hard work,' she said pointedly, before turning to Craig with the most gracious smile she could summon in the circumstances. 'And it's really nice to meet you at last.'

'Likewise.' Craig grinned warmly, his wide smile showing white in the tanned darkness of his face.

He really was a prime specimen of manhood, Miriam thought detachedly as she gazed up into the boyishly attractive face that was topped by a mass of sun-bleached, overlong hair, but although she could appreciate what Barbara found so appealing she had to admit that he left her cold. And when he turned to Barbara, putting his arm about her waist as he pulled her into him, she could see that the handsome Australian had eyes for no one but his bride to be.

'This little lady has been extolling your virtues all the way down here, haven't you, angel?'

'We are grateful, Miriam.' Barbara obviously recognised the impending storm as she glanced at her brother's face again before ushering Craig out of the room quicker than they had come in. 'I'll talk to you tomorrow. I'm just going to fix Craig something to eat.'

'No way.' They heard him laughing as the door began to close. 'I intend to walk down the aisle on my wedding day, angel, not be wheeled down in a chair, suffering from acute food poisoning. Lead me to the kitchen and I'll organise the food.'

'Well?' Reece stared at her for a good few seconds and she willed herself to return the glare without wilting. 'Do they look like the ideal couple to you?'

'Do they have to?' she answered tightly. 'It's what's inside that counts—'

'Don't start that dewy-eyed nonsense on me again,' Reece warned frostily, 'especially after the little display you and the incredible hulk there put on for the rest of us.'

'*What?*' She stared at him in amazement. 'What on earth are you suggesting?'

'I'm not *suggesting* anything,' he countered grimly. 'I'm stating in plain English—which is something else Craig isn't too good at—that he was flirting outrageously and you were encouraging him.'

'I was not,' she shouted indignantly, her voice rising in line with her temper. 'And he was not flirting with me, for goodness' sake; can't you see how much he loves Barbara? He's just friendly, that's all—'

'Oh, he's friendly all right,' Reece answered coldly. 'In fact he's got that particular attribute down to a fine art, and always with the opposite sex from what I can make out.'

'But you don't know him,' she answered incredulously. 'How can you make snap judgements—?'

'I never make snap judgements, but I do have the sort of mind that can sort out the wheat from the chaff instantly,' he said coolly. It was said with such magnificent arrogance, such total disregard for normal, acceptable behaviour, that she didn't know whether to laugh or hit him, but in the end she did the former.

'You really are some sort of megalomaniac.' She smiled scornfully. 'I can't believe you're for real.'

'Believe it, Miriam,' he said darkly, and his mouth moved over hers for a moment, hot and sweet, before he walked briskly out of the room, slamming the door behind him.

CHAPTER SEVEN

THE first thing Miriam noticed as she surfaced from a heavy, troubled sleep the next morning was that her small bedsit was bathed in a quiet, pale glow and the normal morning noise from outside the window was strangely muted.

She lay for some moments in the soft warmth of the bed before steeling herself to move from the comfortable haven into the icy world beyond the covers. The old house was full of draughts and it wasn't at all unusual for the residents to have Jack Frost daub the inside of the windows as well as painting a scene outside.

She padded across to the window and as she pulled back the heavy old velvet curtains, which were more a protection against the sly air currents that permeated the old house than aesthetically attractive, a world of white met her eyes. It had obviously been snowing all night if the thick blanket already covering everything from rooftops to pavements was anything to go by, and still fat white feathery flakes were falling from a laden sky.

It was the last thing she needed at the moment, but in spite of the difficulties the bad weather would undoubtedly bring she stood for a moment just drinking in the magical fairyland outside, the harsh outlines of the bare trees in the small park opposite disguised under their mantle of silvery white.

'Beautiful...' She pushed a strand of silky red hair off her cheek as she breathed her satisfaction before noticing a movement in the street below. And then she froze. Reece Vance was standing looking straight at her window, his face uplifted to the starry flakes, and here was she with just a thin nightie between herself and nakedness.

She stepped back so quickly that she almost brought the curtains with her as her foot caught in the hem of one and the old curtain track groaned protestingly before mercifully deciding to remain in place.

Reece? What on earth was he doing outside her bedsit at this time in the morning? She just had time to run a brush through her hair and fling on her dressing gown before the bell sounded stridently downstairs, and after pushing her feet into the giant monkey slippers that Mitch had bought her for her birthday that year she hurried down, her cheeks flushed and her eyes apprehensive.

'Reece?' She opened the door at once to find him frowning on the doorstep. 'What's wrong?'

'Do you always do that?' he asked testily, without making any effort to step inside.

'Do what?' She stared at him bewilderedly, quite unaware of the warm, glowing picture she made in the doorway, her hair like fire against the white towelling robe and her cheeks flushed and pink.

'Open the door without using that thing?' He gestured to the small intercom fixed to the inside of the hall with its own little security camera enabling the residents to see who was outside when the button was pressed.

'Only sometimes.' She smiled uncertainly as he shook his head grimly. 'I'd already seen you from my window anyway.'

'Miriam, this is the twentieth century in case no one's told you,' he said tightly as he stepped inside the hall, his bulk big and solid against her slimness. 'The landlord was clearly aware of the dangers of a young girl living alone even if you haven't taken them on board.' He looked at her sternly. 'You never, ever open your door again without finding out exactly who is out there. Got it?'

'Reece, I am not exactly a young girl.' She stared up at him as his frown deepened. 'And what are you doing here anyway? It's only seven-thirty in the morning.'

'I'm well aware of the time.' He suddenly seemed faintly embarrassed as he turned and gestured towards the stairs, his voice terse. 'I presume you are going to offer me a cup of coffee on such a filthy morning?'

'When I know why you're here.' She stood her ground so that he was forced to turn and face her again.

'The weather conditions.' He shook his head irritably towards the door. 'The roads are lethal and the rust-bucket isn't too hot at the best of times. I thought it would be a good idea if I came and gave you a lift, especially as you're going to stay for a few days. You can use Barbara's car if you have to go out, but I'd prefer you to get anything you need delivered, OK?'

He turned and began to walk up the stairs. She stared at his departing back as she forced her mind, and her legs, into gear. It didn't mean a thing, not a thing, she told herself harshly as she followed in his footsteps. He was concerned that nothing jeopardised his sister's wedding, that was all, and if there was any kind of complication with herself then things could well grind to a halt. *That was all this meant.*

She had left her door open in her headlong dash downstairs, which earned another frown she chose to ignore. 'Tea or coffee?' she asked brightly as she followed him into the small but cheerful little room she called home.

'Either.' The piercing grey gaze moved swiftly round the room, noticing the bright splashes of colour in the form of a carefully placed pot here, a few gaily bound books there, and came to rest on her watchful face. 'I can see you live here,' he said with a strange element of satisfaction colouring the dark voice. 'It's...provocative to the senses.'

'Is it?' She glanced round the room herself, trying to see it as he would. The curtains were old and faded with age, the carpet threadbare in places which a couple of outrageously coloured rugs hid quite well, but overall the general effect was one of determined cheerfulness in the face of very little money, and quite at odds with the splendour of his home. 'Is that a compliment or an insult?' she asked uncertainly with a faint smile.

'Oh, a compliment, definitely...' He was standing in a shaft of light from the window, and she noticed, before she could shut her mind off from such dangerous thoughts, that he must have shaved recently; his skin was smooth and clean along the hard line of his jaw; it would be silky to the touch.

'I'd better go and change.' As her eyes focused on his she saw a dark heat in their grey depths that reminded her that she had hardly anything on. 'I won't be a minute.'

'Relax, Miriam.' His voice was lazy and confident and she didn't like the way it sent overt little shivers flickering down her spine. 'You're more than decent and I have been with women who were far less clothed without leaping on them. Make us both a drink and then I'll fix some toast while you get changed, OK?'

'You will?' She didn't hide her astonishment quickly enough.

'I will,' he reiterated, with that elusive smile that was so devastating because of its rarity. 'I can actually make toast.' He eyed her sardonically. 'I do quite a mean breakfast, as it happens.'

The wicked gleam in the silver eyes told her that he had set her up for the thought that immediately followed and she flushed hotly as she busied herself filling the kettle and spooning coffee into two china mugs. She just bet he could do breakfast, she thought with bitter jealousy as she wondered how often he had cooked for the woman of the moment. If there was one meal he would be an expert at it would be that one. She filled the mugs savagely.

'I think that's melted.' His dark voice brought her back to the present with a little jolt and she realised that she had been stirring the coffee furiously for a good thirty seconds.

'Sugar and milk?' She glanced at him obliquely, keeping her face and voice bland.

'No, thanks.' He laughed softly, his face sardonic. 'And do go and change if my presence makes you so nervous.'

Nervous? He thought that she was nervous? She wasn't sure if relief dominated the rage his easy assurance produced. Half of her was unutterably thankful that he hadn't guessed her true feelings and the other was furious that he seemed so unmoved when she was a quivering wreck. She drew herself up icily to her full five feet eight inches and fixed him with a cold, blank stare.

'Don't flatter yourself,' she said tightly as the black brows rose mordantly at her coolness. 'I'm just not used to entertaining men in my nightclothes at seven-thirty in the morning, that's all.' She gathered up her clothes and make-up bag in one swoop and marched purposefully to the door. 'Unlike the ladies you normally associate with,' she added for good measure as she banged the door shut behind her and escaped to the bathroom at the end of the corridor on winged feet.

By the time she had showered and changed she was feeling a little more in control. She dressed quickly in jeans and a warm jumper before looping her shiny, silky hair into a high pony-tail at the back of her head and applying a brief touch of mascara to her long dark lashes. There. She glanced at herself in the ancient, misty mirror before leaving the bathroom. If he wanted a glamour puss he could go and find Sharon, but as far as she was concerned this was Miriam Bennett—the original 'what you see is what you get'. She squinted unhappily at the frowning reflection. Or didn't, in his case.

'Scrambled eggs on toast all right?' He turned as she entered the room and her senses went into hyper-drive. He had discarded his coat and jacket and was standing at her minute stove in his shirt-sleeves, stirring the saucepan full of egg while keeping an eye on the toast.

The domestic picture was more than her beleaguered nerves could take and the fact that he looked more gorgeous than any man had the right to at eight o'clock in the morning didn't help. He was doing this on purpose.

She eyed the masculine back suspiciously as she deposited her make-up bag on a shelf. She had agreed—with hindsight, foolishly—that she was physically attracted to him, and this was his way of emphasising what she was missing by sticking to the principles he found so ridiculous.

'Stop frowning,' he said darkly without turning round.

'I wasn't—' She stopped abruptly. She was.

'Honest to the last.' She heard him sigh deeply before whisking the saucepan off the stove, buttering several slices of toast and depositing the lot onto two plates that he had warming on the grill. 'Come and eat this before you explode with self-righteous wrath,' he said mildly as he pushed a plate towards her before seating himself on one of the two stools at the tiny breakfast bar that served as her dining room. 'I have no ulterior motive in being here beyond not wanting you to end up under a lorry,' he added drily as she gingerly took the plate he'd offered. 'Will you please believe that and let us eat this meal in harmony?'

'All right.' She loved him too much to care one way or the other, she thought suddenly as she gave him a radiant smile before she realised what she was doing and seated herself on the other stool. He froze for a long moment before letting the breath out through his teeth in a long hiss and applying himself to the meal.

'Having said that, the situation could alter rapidly if you look at me like that again,' he warned mildly as he glanced at her from under sardonic brows.

He smelt delicious. And he had never been more dangerous than now in this strange mood. 'Like what?' she asked with careful blandness. 'It's OK to smile occasionally, isn't it?' He was too close, far, far too close, perched as they were on these ridiculous stools, she thought helplessly as he turned to face her, grey eyes narrowed, but she couldn't think of an acceptable excuse to move away.

'You smile a lot, don't you?' he drawled lazily as he reached for his coffee-cup and took a long drink, surveying her over the steaming mug thoughtfully. 'Do you really view life with such pleasure?'

'Pleasure?'

Careful, Miriam, careful, she thought weakly as a fierce dart of pain pierced her heart, stopping her breath for a moment. There had been more pain than pleasure lately and it was all down to him.

'I'm not some sort of wind-up doll that bleats happy phrases with a painted smile if that's what you mean,' she said quietly as she reached for her own cup, stirring the dark liquid again to give her hands something to do. 'I've had my share of heartache but I don't believe in wallowing in self-pity; it doesn't help anyone and it's self-destructive.'

Are you listening to this, Miriam? she asked herself with bitter irony as she glanced up. You're going to have to remember this conversation when the final goodbye is over.

'I asked you once if you'd ever loved someone—a man,' he said softly as she looked down into the swirling coffee again. 'And you never did give me a straight answer.'

'Didn't I?' She drew a long, shuddering breath as her mind raced. What could she say to him? How could she answer this? In the end the truth seemed simpler than trying to lie. 'I've been in love,' she said briefly. 'Unfortunately it wasn't returned so that was the end of the story.'

'Wasn't returned?' She dared not look at his face but his voice was odd, tight and strained. 'The guy must have been mad.'

He is, she thought blindly as she forced herself to pick up her knife and fork as though her world wasn't falling apart around her ears and eat the scrambled eggs on toast calmly, pushing the food painfully through the massive lump in her throat. Mad and wonderful and hateful and everything I want. She shrugged lightly but said nothing.

'And that experience didn't make you bitter, even for a time?' he asked after a long moment. 'If you thought you loved him—'

'I didn't *think* anything,' she said unsteadily as she climbed down from the stool and took her plate to the tiny kitchen area. 'I told you before, love is a real emotion that does exist. It isn't always comfortable, or even welcome, but that doesn't make it any less real. It would be nice if everything worked out exactly how we want it every time but life's not like that.'

'Miriam?' She hadn't been aware that he had followed her but now, feeling his hand on her shoulder, she steeled herself to show no emotion as she turned to face him. 'You're very lovely and very brave—and, I repeat, that guy was a fool.' He made no attempt to touch her further, for which she was supremely grateful—one more word, one more gentle pat and she would either have hit him or burst into tears, neither of which would have served any purpose.

His mouth was straight and tight, his eyes pure silver and as sharp as glass—he was clearly furious with this man who had spurned her affections. As well he might be, she thought with a sudden burst of rage that gave her the strength to shrug lightly and turn back to the washing-up.

They left the house some ten minutes later, Reece carrying her case in one hand and holding onto her arm with the other as he led her over the thick snow to his car. He had hardly said two words since their conversation over breakfast, retreating into a dark, distant mood that Miriam made no attempt to lighten. She felt bruised and raw and desperately sad, and more unhappy than she had ever been in her life.

She glanced at him now as he slid into the car beside her, the hard, masculine face taut and remote, the silver eyes as cold as ice. Sharon would fit into his world perfectly; there was no doubt about that. From the little she had seen of the beautiful blonde she thought that Sharon would be exactly what Reece wanted her to be whenever he wanted it—a lovely living doll to play all the right parts at the right time.

The drive to his house was more hazardous than she had expected, the thick white flakes of snow falling so quickly that the windscreen wipers had difficulty clearing them and the roads lethal with packed snow, huge drifts already mounting either side of the verges.

'Barbara's going to panic.'

As they drew into the long drive she breathed a sigh of relief that the journey had been completed without any mishap and turned to Reece quietly. 'It won't last, and better today than on the actual wedding day.' She touched his arm tentatively as he cut the ignition. 'And thanks for turning out on a morning like this, Reece; I hadn't realised it was so bad. Perhaps my car wouldn't have made it after all, but I could have got a taxi. You shouldn't have come yourself.'

'Yes, I should.' In the infinitesimal moment of time that he looked at her before opening the car door she saw something in his face that made her heart leap into her throat, but then, as he walked round the bonnet and helped her out, she saw that his features were remote and cold, his eyes hooded. 'Have you seen how some of those taxi drivers drive?' he asked drily. 'The chances of you arriving here in one piece to soothe Barbara's ruffled feathers were highly remote.'

He had parked just outside the door leading to the kitchens, and after opening the boot and extracting her case he followed her into the corridor, walking through to the flat's front door, whereupon he put down the case and delved into his pocket for the key.

'You've got a key on your keyring as well,' he said
shortly as he opened the door and placed the case just
inside. 'And there's a bolt on the front door too, once
you're settled down for the night.' He eyed her expressionlessly. 'Just so you feel doubly safe,' he added
enigmatically before turning and walking back the way
they had come.

She stood quietly for a moment or two, hearing his
car start and drive away round to the front of the house,
and breathed out slowly, her heart thudding.

She had imagined that expression on his face before
he opened the car door—a look of hunger and deep
emotion that echoed something in her own heart. He
had made it perfectly clear this morning in everything
he'd said and done that he had come to fetch her in
order to ensure that the next few days ran as smoothly
as possible. Barbara was all that mattered to him, she
knew that—she *knew* it, so why did her traitorous heart
keep hoping for something more? She shook her head
blindly. And now he'd got her imagining things too. She
really would end up in a strait-jacket before this little
lot was through if she wasn't careful.

She took a long, deep, tortured breath and forced
herself to pick up the case and walk through to the small
bedroom, where she began to pack away her few clothes
methodically. He'd employed her to do a job, nothing
more. If she had been game for a little light affair at the
same time then that would have been a bonus for him,
but that was all it would have been. His heart was encased in ice and likely to remain that way until someone
far more experienced in the ways of life and love than
she had the opportunity to break through.

Once the unpacking was finished she walked through
to the kitchens to begin work, forcing her mind to concentrate on the job in hand. Mitch and the others were
due to arrive about nine, but with the weather conditions set against them they could well be late. She was
going to have to work like crazy even to maintain a sem-

blance of the schedule they had worked out so carefully. She shook her head irritably. This job had been doomed from the start.

Nine came and went, followed by a phone call from Mitch a few minutes later. 'Mim?' Her brother's voice was harassed. 'This has thrown us into one hell of a mess, hasn't it?'

'Not at all.' She slipped back into her accustomed role of comforter and optimist even as something deep inside rebelled suddenly. She wanted someone to help *her*, talk positively and firmly and take the burden off *her* shoulders. And she wasn't thinking of this damn job either, she added with silent bitterness.

'I've just cleared the drive here at home and phoned Vera and Dave to tell them to let everyone know I'll pick them up in the van,' Mitch continued quickly. 'At least the van's got a better chance of getting through than several cars. We should be with you about ten if you can hold the fort till then.'

'Fine. I won't be twiddling my thumbs for something to do,' she added wryly.

She decided to pop through to the main house to tell Mrs Goode when the others were going to arrive and check when the agency staff were due. Reece had employed three women to help Mrs Goode and Jinny in the main house in view of the number of guests who would be staying over for the weekend and, as long as they arrived, along with the extra hands that Mitch had arranged for the actual wedding day, they should be able to cope.

Jinny, under Mrs Goode's direction, had prepared the main hall the day before and it was ready now except for the fresh flowers due to be put in place early on Saturday morning. Miriam glanced at the walls festooned with ribbon and horseshoes as she crossed the immaculate floor and felt a pang in her heart region as she contemplated how lucky Barbara and Craig were to have found each other despite all the odds stacked against

them. Theirs was a love match if ever she had seen one—
a meeting of two souls who complemented each other
perfectly in spite of being totally different.

She heard the raised voices before she had even gone
through the door leading into the main house, and once
in the hall outside she recognised that a furious row was
in progress. She took a few uncertain steps before hesi-
tating halfway down the hall. Reece's voice was clearly
identifiable, although not his actual words, and who the
unfortunate individual facing him was she had no idea.

The next moment the door to the drawing room burst
open and Craig emerged, his face as white as a sheet as
he took the stairs two at a time, disappearing upstairs.

'I'll never forgive you for this—never.' Barbara's voice
was quivering with rage but as cold as ice as she, too,
appeared in the doorway, her back to Miriam as she faced
Reece, who was still inside the room. 'I hate you. Do
you hear me? I hate you!'

'There's is no need for such hysterics.' She could imagine how infuriating Barbara found the coolly angry
reply, and as Reece's sister's back stiffened she waited
for the explosion to follow.

'You insinuate that Craig doesn't really love me, that
he's after my money, and then follow that with the idea
that I'm marrying him on a whim to satisfy some strange
biological urge, and you tell me there's no need for hysterics!' Barbara screamed at the top of her voice. 'How
dare you? How dare you, Reece? What gives you the
right to think you know how Craig or I feel?'

'I merely asked if it was necessary to make your relationship legal,' Reece said with icy stiffness. 'Situations change, people change. In a few months' time
you might feel quite differently, and then you'll have a
huge financial settlement to think about if you want to
finish the marriage.'

'I shan't want to finish the marriage!'

Well, that was definite, Miriam thought faintly as she closed her eyes against Reece's blundering. Oh, Reece, you fool, she thought helplessly. You blind, stupid fool.

'You've ruined it all now and it was to be the best day of my life. Craig's going to a hotel and we've got all his relations arriving tomorrow— Oh!' Barbara stamped her feet as she literally ground her teeth at him. 'I really hate you at this moment, Reece; I wish you'd never been born.' And then she was gone, flying up the stairs after Craig as she burst into a storm of weeping that rocked the house.

Miriam waited for a minute or two and then crept tentatively to the open door. Reece was standing with his back to the room, looking out of the huge windows into the cold white world outside, his body stiff and taut and his hands thrust deep into his trouser pockets.

'Reece?' As she spoke his name he swung round immediately, his face as black as thunder.

'I suppose you heard all that?' he said bitterly. 'I should think everyone from here to Land's End could hear it.'

'You're wrong, you know,' she said very quietly as she came fully into the room and closed the door behind her. 'Barbara loves him very much and I'm sure he feels the same. Your sister is the type of person who only loves once and then she gives it her all. Craig is the man for her, whatever happens. I should imagine your father was the same from what you've told me.'

'You know nothing about it.' There was a stricken look to his face that pained her. Clearly the bitter quarrel with his twin had hurt him more than he would admit. 'Dammit, you've only met Barbara a couple of times; how can you possibly give a judgement on something like this?'

'Probably because I *have* only met her recently,' Miriam said carefully. 'You're too close to it all to recognise what's happened beneath your very nose. You had always imagined she was like you, content with a high-powered career and taking her fun where she found it with no thoughts of settling down. And probably until she met Craig that was how she did think. But not now. And he isn't what you think. That first time you met him he was ill, suffering from jet lag, not drunk and mauling some girl, although I know it looked like that.'

'It seems as if you *know* a damn sight too much,' he said bitterly.

'Just listen for a moment.' She walked across the room to stand in front of him, wondering what on earth she could say to make him see the truth. 'I know your parents' marriage wasn't particularly happy, that they shut you and Barbara out—'

'My mother made my father's life a living hell,' he said tightly, his mouth a thin white line in the hard planes of his face. 'He turned cartwheels to make her happy, to give her what she wanted, but nothing was good enough. She couldn't be bothered with Barbara and me so he sent us away on the pretext of giving us a good education. He showered her with jewellery, presents, holidays abroad—anything she wanted—and lived in the dread that one day she would meet someone else she could love and leave him. But he needn't have worried; she was incapable of any deep emotion—a beautiful, empty shell of a human being.'

'Perhaps every generation throws up one or two anomalies.' She desperately wanted to hold him, to kiss away the pain and hurt transparent on his face, but forced herself to continue speaking in a calm, flat tone to try and defuse the crackling tension. 'Unnatural women or men, abnormal and strange and a law unto themselves, but unless they are blessed with either great wealth or great beauty I guess they get unnoticed in the general rush of life. But they *are* unnatural. Your mother was unnatural—'

'Perhaps.' The silver eyes fastened on her pale face. 'But with a heritage like that Barbara and Craig have got no chance.'

'That's just plain stupid,' she snapped angrily as his stubbornness hit a nerve. 'You can take what life dishes out and either let it make you bitter or learn from it and go on to the next chapter.

'Barbara went through the same problems as you did but she has chosen to put it behind her and reach out for the happiness she knows she can have with Craig. Just because you haven't got the courage to accept that, you are in great danger of losing her for ever, Reece. She is too much like you to make empty threats, and if you don't stop this thing now, make amends before the sun goes down and accept Craig simply because she loves him and he is her choice, you'll regret it for the rest of your life.'

'Little Miss Set-the-world-to-rights.'

His mockery was scathing, and the final straw. Her hand shot out as if to slap his face, but dropped to her side at the last moment. She saw his eyes darken with rage before he grabbed her, forcing her head back as he took her lips in a bruising kiss that stopped her breath. She began to fight him, causing them both to lose their balance and fall sprawling onto the big leather settee at their side, Reece's body covering hers as they landed.

And still she fought him, desperately, silently, as waves and waves of hurt and anger and love flooded her mind and body until she was hardly lucid. And then, as he continued the assault on her senses by shifting tempo as he trapped her body with his, she knew that this was a fight she couldn't win. Because she loved him; even in the midst of her pain and anger she loved him. Whereas he was driven by a simple physical need that had no warmth, no real tenderness in the heart of it. He didn't *care*. The knowledge gave her the strength she needed to speak.

'Please stop.' She opened her eyes that had been shut tight to stare straight into the grey of his, their smokiness hot with desire. 'Please.'

He froze for one second before moving off her in a single, controlled movement that spoke of quiet rage, and she slid quickly to her feet and across the room before he could speak, pulling open the door and running down the hall as though her life depended on it.

Once in the kitchens she leant weakly against the wall, shocked beyond measure by the suddenness of the confrontation. There was a mountain of work to do, but as her eyes focused unseeingly on the Christmas-card scene outside the window all her mind and energy was centred on Reece.

He *had* to make things all right with Barbara, she thought desperately. It would hurt him more than he knew if he lost his sister. She shook her head blindly at her own stupidity. She shouldn't have argued with him, shouldn't have allowed the conversation to progress as it had. It had only served to make him more mad, and she had gone into the room with the purpose of calming things down!

She groaned out loud and walked unsteadily to the coffee-maker which she had left switched on, pouring herself a large mug of black coffee—something she never drank—and forcing herself to drink it down piping hot as she tried to make her mind a blank. She had too much work to do to brood—although whether the wedding was still on, and whether Barbara would be married from this house, were points suddenly worryingly unclear.

Why did Reece have to be so honest anyway? She rubbed her hand across her face shakily and picked up the list of jobs she had made the night before. Why couldn't he duck and dive a little, like the rest of the human race? But then that was one of the things she loved about him, she thought sadly as she began to check the ingredients for the vol-au-vents she intended to make—that devastatingly scrupulous honesty.

Mitch and the others arrived just after ten as the snow began to lessen into the occasional flake blown haphazardly in the chilly wind, and soon the kitchen was a hive of activity. She didn't mention the earlier scene to Mitch—somehow it would have seemed like a form of disloyalty to Reece and Barbara—and she knew that if the worst happened, and Barbara decided not to come back to the house after she was married, Reece would make sure that the financial arrangements were honoured.

Please don't let that happen, she prayed desperately as her hands worked methodically on. He would be devastated if he lost Barbara; she knew it. In spite of his protestations about love and deep emotion she knew that he cared deeply about his sister; even the fact that he had raised the matter with Barbara and Craig proved that.

It would have been far easier, and safer, to sit back and allow the thing to happen and then pick up the pieces at a later date if the need arose. But he was so *stubborn*. The knife she was holding slipped at the thought and she just avoided slicing into her finger. And so was Barbara. This sort of incident was the stuff family feuds were born of.

She shook her head and forced herself to concentrate on the job in hand as the bustle and noise ebbed and flowed around her. It would work out—it had to—and anyway, as Reece had reminded her, none of this was anything to do with her. She set her heart against the hurt and pain that gripped it and began slicing the peppers she was preparing with fierce determination.

'Miriam?' They had been working steadily for over an hour and a half and were just enjoying a midday snack when she heard Reece's voice from the doorway. 'Could I have a word, please?'

'Sure.' She forced a polite smile for the sake of the others and rose quickly. She could read nothing from his face as she followed him into the corridor and shut the kitchen door firmly. His features could have been set in stone for all the emotion they betrayed.

'I want to apologise for the way I behaved earlier,' he said grimly as he stared down at her fixedly, his face rigid and taut. 'It was unforgivable—'

'Oh, no. You were upset,' she broke in quickly, her voice too high. 'I shouldn't have interfered; I know that, but—'

'Miriam, let me say what I have to say without you trying to exonerate the inexcusable.' He took a long, deep breath as though he found her overwhelmingly exasperating, and she lowered her eyes quickly as a little shaft of pain pierced her through. 'Not that I don't appreciate it.' His voice was a study in icy control. 'But I was way out of line when all you were trying to do was help. I've seen Barbara and Craig—' her gaze shot up to his face and clung there, wide-eyed '—and we've been talking for more than an hour. You were right, Miriam; I think they really do have something going for them.'

'You do?' The relief almost made her giddy. 'You told them that?'

He nodded slowly. 'I extended the olive branch and Craig was gracious enough to accept it so all is peace and harmony again, OK? So there's nothing for you to worry about. You *were* worrying, weren't you?' he added softly. She nodded quietly and his mouth twisted slightly. 'Well, you can stop now. Barbara is going to marry her prince and live happily ever after. I haven't ruined things for her.'

I wasn't worrying about *Barbara*, she told him silently as she gazed up into his dark face. At this moment I couldn't care less about Barbara and Craig or the whole caboodle—can't you see that? Are you really so blind?

'Thank you, Miriam.' His voice was so quiet now that she was almost lip-reading, but the look on his face rent her heart. 'I know you were concerned about Barbara but you stopped me from making the biggest mistake of my life. I didn't want to hurt her, you know, or either of them.'

'I know.' She could hardly get the whisper past the lump in her throat.

He nodded slowly, almost dragging his eyes from her face as he backed a step before turning and walking swiftly up the corridor to disappear through the door at the top into the hall.

Oh, Reece. She leant against the wall as hot tears flowed fast and salty down her face. Reece, Reece, Reece...

CHAPTER EIGHT

IN SPITE of her emotional turmoil, sheer physical exhaustion guaranteed that Miriam was asleep as soon as her head touched the pillow that night. Mitch and the others had stayed until ten, which meant that everything was back on schedule. She had planned to have the freezers full, the fridges stocked and most of the preliminary work completed that night, leaving Friday free for setting up the big hall and the thousand and one last-minute preparations essential in a massive undertaking like this.

She slept deeply, to dream frantic dreams involving giant wedding cakes with two legs that ran away as soon as they were about to be cut, hundreds of guests arriving to no food and an empty hall, Barbara screaming and fighting Craig as she shouted that Reece had been right all along and she didn't want to get married, and, over all the tangled, weary mess, the brooding presence of a tall, silent man breathed dark confusion and despair.

Waking was a sweet relief, and Miriam sat eating her breakfast at six o'clock as she gazed out of the window into a garden transformed into a sparkling winter wonderland, unable to bear staying in that dark, nightmarish world a minute longer.

A host of birds were pottering hopefully on top of the thick snow, darting bright, inquisitive glances at the house and fluttering onto the frozen birdbath now and again in search of a drink. They couldn't have made a more pointed request for food, and Miriam dressed quickly after defrosting a loaf of bread in the microwave and filling a large container with hot water.

As she opened the door at the end of the corridor the cold air made her gasp, and she stood for a moment breathing in the icy sweetness before plodding round the side of the house with her gifts. The early-morning sky was a river of gold and pink, colouring the snow with a luminescent quality all its own, and everything was quiet and absolutely still.

After melting the ice Miriam filled the birdbath with clean water, which lay gently steaming in the freezing air, and then cleared a patch of ground for the bread, scattering small pieces in a wide circle before moving away to a snow-covered bench at the side of a large bush and brushing herself a seat.

She sat for a long time watching the birds feed as the sky changed to a pearly white, not thinking of anything but the scene in front of her and letting the quiet peace of the morning blanket her mind. She pulled the hood of her old duffle-coat even further over her face as the icy air began to freeze her nose, and then jumped violently as a deep male voice sounded just a few feet away.

'What on earth are you doing out here?' She looked over to where Reece was standing and felt the familiar jolt to her heart as she took in the sight of him in the clear crystal air. He was dressed in jeans and a waist-length, bulky grey jacket, its collar up round his neck and his head bare to the elements. His impressive height and lean body were accentuated in the pale white surroundings, his maleness a tangible thing as his eyes narrowed in enquiry.

'Nothing.' She indicated the birds who had scattered at his voice and were now fluttering back in ones and twos. 'The birds were hungry.'

He raised his hands and she noticed for the first time that he was carrying a large fruit-cake and a container of water. 'I know.' He smiled ruefully. 'The little blighters are used to their morning feed. I think they'd come knocking on the door if I was late.'

'You feed them every day?' she asked in surprise as a warning bell began to ring in her mind. Don't do this to me, she thought silently as she watched him smile that heart-stoppingly attractive smile before walking over to join her. I don't want to find out fresh things to make me love you more; I can't cope as it is. I don't want to know that you are capable of caring about hungry birds; this just isn't *fair*.

'In the winter.' He sat down beside her on the bench and she felt her body tense at his closeness as he stretched out his long legs in front of him. 'In the summer they fend for themselves.' He glanced at her, his eyes reflecting the silver-white sky overhead. 'You look like Little Red Riding Hood in that get-up.'

'Except it's brown.' She smiled unsteadily and then her heart thumped crazily as he raised a lazy hand and flicked back her hood, causing her hair to tumble about her shoulders.

'Now it's red.' He lifted a handful of thick, silky hair in his fingers and rubbed each strand thoughtfully as it slipped back to settle in soft waves around her face. 'You're beautiful, Miriam, so beautiful. How many men have told you that?' She stared at him unblinkingly, unable to speak. 'Did *he* tell you how lovely you are?' he asked with sudden roughness.

'Who?'

'The guy you loved.' The sudden heat that flooded her face brought his mouth into a tight, straight line. 'Or is it *love*?' he asked grimly. 'Do you still care for this moron, Miriam? Is that why you don't want anything to do with me?'

'Reece—' She put out a hand almost placatingly as she stood up abruptly. She could take most things with a smile but this was beyond her. 'I don't want to talk about it.'

'I could make you forget him.' He stood with her, his height and breadth intimidating as he looked down at her, his handsome face fierce and harsh. 'You know we could be good together; you feel it like I do.'

'You're talking about physical gratification,' she said flatly as she moved round him in one quick movement and began to walk away. 'I could never be satisfied with that.'

'You might find you actually like me too,' he said tightly, but she didn't look back, walking at a steady pace until she rounded the side of the house and slipped inside quickly. The sooner this wedding was over the better.

She stood for a long minute just inside the corridor before walking to the flat door. Seeing him like this, knowing that he wanted her if only for a casual affair— she couldn't take much more of it...

She walked over to the window as soon as she was in the flat, drawn against her will to see if he was still out there. He was, his bulk dark and dangerous against the pure white garden as he crumbled the cake for the squabbling birds and refilled the birdbath they had all but emptied.

Why oh, why had Frank ever recommended them for this job? she asked herself weakly as she moved away from the window and leant helplessly against the wall. She'd been doing fine, happy with her life and eager for the future, and now... She shut her eyes tightly and breathed deeply to ease her racing heart. Now she'd never be the same again. She would never love anyone the way she loved him. She knew it. Reece Vance only happened to a girl once.

The day flew by in a whirl of frenzied chaos that wasn't enhanced by the arrival of Craig's relations *en masse* just after lunch. They seemed a loud, noisy lot, if the general furore beyond the walls of the hall was anything to go by, and as Mitch and Dave arranged the tables and chairs at her direction to allow plenty of room for dancing she couldn't help wondering, with a wry smile, what Reece thought of the merry throng.

Several of the guests had wandered through with Craig and Barbara as they'd looked round the house, and now the door leading to the house opened again and Reece entered with a small party of Australians in tow, a pained expression on his face as he acted the benevolent host.

'This is the big hall.' He waved a hand expressively. 'The caterers are busy at it so we won't interrupt them.'

'Hi, there.' One of the party had a different idea, and the eyes of a big, tall, blond man, who could have been Craig's double, fastened interestedly on Miriam's slender form. 'You look like you have everything under control here.'

'We do.' She smiled back politely and immediately he ambled over to her side, his blue eyes bright and smiling and his teeth the sort of gleaming white that would have done credit to any toothpaste advertisement.

'The name's Donnie.' He held out a massive hand for her to shake. 'I'm over from Australia for the wedding.'

'Right.' She nodded quietly, vitally aware of Reece's frowning face in the background but unable to do anything else but respond civilly to the Australian's friendly chatter.

'You arranged all this, then?' He waved an expansive hand round the hall as he kept his eyes trained on her face.

She smiled awkwardly. 'My brother and I are partners in the firm Mr Vance employed.'

'Oh, yeh, that's right.' He nodded quickly. 'Craig, my brother, told me about the trouble with the other bozos. Reece was lucky to find you at such short notice.' His eyes wandered over the burning red of her hair and came to rest in line with her quiet gaze. 'Very lucky,' he added softly.

'I think we're in the way here.' Reece's voice was pure ice as he appeared at their side. 'It's clear there's still plenty of work to be done, so if you'd like to...' He gestured towards the door through which they'd just passed, his face grim.

'No problem.' Donnie turned from Reece to smile at her again. 'I guess you'll be here tomorrow too?'

'Oh, yes.' She grimaced ruefully. 'You won't see me for dust as I race about, though.'

'I wouldn't bank on that.' He nodded at Mitch and the others, who had stopped work to watch the little scenario with purposely blank faces, and followed Reece and the rest of the party towards the door, stopping in the doorway as he turned back to her with a little exclamation. 'Hey, I forgot to ask your name.'

'Miriam Bennett.' As Reece loomed back over his shoulder she felt something akin to a giggle begin to surface and bit it back quickly. Here was one man who wasn't the least intimidated by Reece Vance's threatening coolness.

'Miriam...' He nodded slowly in approval. 'It suits you; very feminine.'

'If you're ready...?' As Reece almost pushed him out of the way and began to shut the door he sent Miriam a glance of cold fury that she was at a loss to understand. 'I'd carry on working if I were you,' he said tightly as he disappeared. 'It looks to me like there's still a lot to be done.'

'Ignorant pig!' She turned back to the others with an angry shake of her head as her cheeks burnt hotly. 'What on earth does he think we're going to do if not work?'

'The guy's under a lot of pressure,' Mitch said soothingly as he and Dave began to unfold one of the huge white linen tablecloths and lay it across the table that they were standing behind. 'I should imagine he works on a short fuse at the best of times, and having his house invaded by an army of strangers and turned upside down by us can't be much fun for the poor chap.'

'Huh!' Reece's cold face and tight voice had hurt her more than what he had actually said, but she forced herself to put it out of her mind as they began work again. Two or three days and she'd never see him again, so what did any of it matter?

The thought sent her heart plummeting to her feet as a great sense of desolation overwhelmed her. She had had the chance to have more of him, but where would his lovemaking have led in the end? To a broken heart. She didn't just want his body, she wanted much, much more, and giving herself to him would have meant that she was intrinsically linked with him; it *would*—that was just the way she was made.

She sighed deeply, unaware of Mitch's intuitive eyes watching her face. She couldn't have walked away from him when the time came for him to dismiss her and the whole thing would have got painfully messy, humiliating and embarrassing for them both. He would have guessed how she felt in time; she never had been very good at hiding her feelings. No. She had done the right thing, the only thing, but it hurt like mad. And she had the horrible feeling that it always would.

'Mim?' Mitch appeared at her side as the others worked at the far end of the hall. 'It could never work, you know. You *do* know that?'

'What?' Miriam turned to him as she felt herself flush bright red.

'It's obvious he fancies you,' Mitch said softly. 'And give me a bit of credit for having known you for the last twenty-five years. You've fallen for him, haven't you?'

'Mitch—' She stopped abruptly, not wanting to offend him as she noticed the look of deep concern on his face. 'I really don't want to discuss this, OK? There's no chance of my getting involved with him; death wishes aren't my style, all right?'

'You're sure about that?' Mitch asked quietly. She nodded quickly, her face bleak, and then sniffed dismally as her brother hugged her hard. 'Good girl.' He wagged his head as he imitated a line from one of their favourite TV programmes. 'You know it makes sense. And soon all this will just be history.'

'Yes.' He was trying to help but failing miserably, and she worked like a beaver for the rest of the day, forcing herself on until she was ready to drop.

Mitch and the others disappeared home just after five but she worked on until six in the kitchen, laying out the utensils and dishes needed to prepare the fresh salads and sauces, and then walked through to the flat for a long, hot bath and an early night.

She needed to be up at five the next morning, Mitch and the others were arriving at six, and by the end of tomorrow it would all be over. The agency staff had taken over in the main house—she knew that Mrs Goode had arranged a formal dinner for eight o'clock—but as far as she was concerned the only thing that held any appeal was her bed.

She lay for over an hour in the warm, soapy water, adding fresh bubbles whenever the others dispersed, and, after washing her hair, climbed out and swaddled herself in a huge bathsheet while she ate a simple meal of cheese on toast followed by fresh fruit. She felt exhausted and drained, but mercifully it seemed to have numbed her mind, and when she fell into bed, at just after eight, she sank immediately into a deep, dreamless sleep which made it all the more difficult to surface two hours later to the relentless knocking on her front door.

She stumbled through to the lounge after pulling her robe tightly round her, more asleep than awake, and opened the door in a daze. 'Yes?' It took her a few seconds to focus and then she saw Reece's dark, angry face a few inches from her own. 'What's wrong?'

'Wrong?' He smiled nastily as he brushed past her into the flat without so much as a by-your-leave. 'Why should anything be wrong?'

'Reece!' She was instantly and furiously awake as she watched him walk through and give a cursory glance at the small bedroom before coming back into the lounge. 'What on earth do you think you're doing? I'm tired, I've got to be up early in the morning and I haven't got time to play guessing-games. What do you want?'

'I thought—' He stopped abruptly and she was surprised to see a dark stain of red colour on the high male cheekbones. 'Were you asleep?' he prevaricated flatly.

'Of course I was asleep.' She brushed her hair back from her face as she took in his big dark body in a formal dinner suit that made him look like all her Christmases rolled into one. 'And, for the third time, what's wrong?'

'It was just that—' He stopped again. 'Oh, hell...' He rubbed his hand across his face and looked at her with narrowed eyes. 'Donnie wasn't around and no one seemed to know where he was, and I just thought—'

'You thought he was here with me?' she asked in tones of absolute amazement. 'Why—?' She shook her head angrily. 'No, don't answer that. Surely you knew I wouldn't encourage a virtual stranger in here last thing at night? It's not even my flat, for goodness' sake.'

'You didn't do a bad job of encouraging him this morning,' he said tightly as he gazed into her angry violet eyes. 'From where I was standing it seemed the two of you were hitting it off just fine.'

'Well, you were obviously standing in the wrong place, then,' she snapped back furiously. 'And, anyway, what gives you the right to barge in here all guns firing without even checking your facts? I wouldn't dream of asking one of your guests in here. It would be totally unethical. I am your employee after all.'

'And that's why you wouldn't ask him in, because it's unethical?' he asked grimly as he scowled at her darkly.

'That and other reasons.' She drew herself up proudly, although the effect was somewhat diminished by the voluminous towelling robe that had always been a couple of sizes too big.

'Like?'

'Like I don't know the man, I don't *want* to know the man, and I don't happen to be the sort of woman to put myself in a precarious position with someone I've just met,' she said angrily. 'For goodness' sake, Reece!' She shut her eyes for a moment as sheer hot rage flooded her limbs. 'What exactly do you think I am?'

'Gorgeous.' All the darkness had left his face as she had spoken and now the deep, husky quality of his voice sent her nerves jumping as she looked up into his eyes. 'Unbelievably gorgeous. What about someone you haven't just met?' he asked softly.

'What?'

'Would they be allowed in? Just for a cup of coffee?' he asked humbly. She stared at him suspiciously. Reece Vance breathing fire and damnation was one thing, but in this conciliatory, meek mood? He was ten times more dangerous.

'I don't think—'

'Just a cup of coffee and then I'll go,' he smiled disarmingly.

It was the smile that did it. She saw it so rarely that it melted her resistance like bright sun on ice, and she knew that he'd won. He knew it too. His smile widened and he moved to close the door that was still open. 'I'll have mine black,' he said lazily as he sprawled out on the small sofa in the lounge. 'And I really am very sorry, Miriam. I just didn't want Donnie...bothering you in any way.'

'He hasn't,' she said shortly as she walked through to the kitchen and took a long, deep breath to calm her racing heartbeat. Dammit, she was playing with fire here.

This was a ridiculous situation and she should never have put herself in such a position—

'You look lovely when you've just woken up.' He had come to lean lazily against the kitchen door, watching her with keen, hooded eyes as she fumbled about in the cupboards for coffee and sugar. 'I knew you would.'

She must look a mess, she thought helplessly as she ignored his words and concentrated on the mundane. 'Is instant all right?' she asked flatly, keeping the tremor out of her voice with superhuman resolve. 'I haven't really got time to make proper coffee; I've got to be up very early in the morning.'

'Haven't we all...?' Her remark seemed to draw him back onto safer lines. 'Barbara's skittering about like a chicken with its head cut off, Mrs Goode is having one panic attack after another, my house has been invaded by aliens who seem to speak a totally different language from me—' He sighed deeply. 'I shall be damn glad when this wedding is over.'

When it's over? His words pierced her heart like a sword and she was desperately glad that her back was to him as she spooned coffee into two mugs and added sugar in hers with a shaking hand. 'I suppose you will,' she said carefully, when she could trust her voice again. 'It's never the most relaxed of times.' When it's over I shan't see you again, she screamed silently as she added water to the coffee and stirred vigorously. But you don't care; you've never really cared. *How can you want it over?*

She handed him his coffee when she turned round, and as they walked through to the lounge she warned herself for the umpteenth time to be careful. She had to keep this on a purely friendly level, she mustn't let him touch her—

'Sit down by me.' He patted the sofa as he flung himself down, but she smiled carefully as she seated herself on one of the chairs, sitting on the edge with her feet neatly together and pulling the robe firmly over her legs.

'Spoilsport...' He smiled lazily and her heart flipped over again. This was a seduction technique; it had to be. Two smiles in as many minutes wasn't natural for Reece! 'Where on earth did you get those things from, by the way?' he asked idly as he gestured towards her massive monkey slippers which were quite grotesque.

'Mitch.' She smiled her first natural smile since he had arrived. 'Ridiculous, aren't they?'

'Unusual.' He fiddled with his bow-tie and then set down his coffee-cup. 'Do you mind?' he asked mildly as he gestured towards the tight collar. 'This thing's killing me.'

'Of course not.' Oh, help, she thought silently.

He undid his collar and pulled the tie loose to hang down in two black strands as he opened the top few buttons of his shirt. She couldn't handle this, she really couldn't. She could just see dark, curling body hair at the top of his shirt where his chest was revealed, and as her stomach muscles clenched and a slow, sweet throb took over her pulse she was shocked at her body's animal response to his maleness. She wanted him—she wanted him so badly that she could taste it; she licked suddenly dry lips and took a quick gulp of coffee to ease her aching throat.

'You're very transparent.' His voice was thick suddenly, and husky, with a deepness that set her senses tingling. 'You're petrified I'm going to leap on you, aren't you—force you to the floor and have my wicked way with you?'

He thought that she was nervous? She breathed a sigh of relief and forced herself to look at him. It wasn't nerves that were strangling her voice and freezing her limbs but the knowledge that if the iron hold she had over herself slipped she'd fly at him and eat him alive.

'Not at all.' She smiled shakily.

'Little liar.' He eyed her mockingly. 'I can always tell the very rare occasions that you lie because it doesn't come naturally to you, does it? That's just one of the things that has amazed me about you, Miriam; I hadn't reckoned to meet someone like you in several lifetimes.' He laughed suddenly, but the sound was harsh in the quiet room. 'Looking like you do and still a virgin at twenty-five. Do you know that you are probably unique in the whole of London?' he asked with wry, caustic humour.

'I doubt it.' She blushed scarlet.

'You can trust me, you know,' he said after a long moment. 'I know you think I'm the lowest thing on two legs but I wouldn't take you against your will; not even I would stoop to that,' he added bitterly.

Against my will? She would have laughed out loud if it had been possible. Two seconds after he touched her it sure wouldn't be against her will, she thought with painful self-contempt.

'What is it exactly that you object to so strongly?' he asked softly, after another pause that she found impossible to break. 'I know on a sexual level we would be compatible; you know it too.'

'We're so different...' She couldn't believe how near she was to blurting out the truth; it was quivering on her tongue like a live thing, and only the knowledge that he would take her love and use it against her kept her from admitting the truth. He had told her that he didn't want to love a woman and she knew him well enough by now to know that what he didn't want to do, he didn't. He was cynical and cold and cruelly honest and he just wanted to get her into bed. *Remember it*, she told herself fiercely.

'Sunday's child can get on with anyone,' he reminded her lightly.

'Not really.' She glanced up at him suddenly. 'What day were you born on, Reece?'

'What?' He looked at her blankly for a moment and then shook his head slowly. 'A Wednesday, I think. Yes, a Wednesday.' He eyed her wryly. 'Is that good or bad?'

'"Wednesday's child is full of woe."' She took another long sip of coffee. 'I don't think Sunday is ready to meet Wednesday yet,' she said flatly as she placed her mug on the table by her side.

'Sunday doesn't know what it's missing.' He moved so swiftly that she didn't have time to object as he pulled her to her feet and into his arms, kissing her passionately as he moulded her into the hard length of him.

She shuddered helplessly as his warm lips moved down over her throat, their touch tantalisingly sensuous. Quite whether the robe fell apart or he moved it apart she wasn't sure, but as his mouth burnt on the soft swell of her breasts a moment later the pleasure she felt drowned all thoughts of protest.

'I want you, Miriam; I've wanted you from the first moment I set eyes on you.' His eyes were silver slits in the dark passion of his face. 'I can't think of anything else. I'm becoming obsessed with you and I hate feeling like it but I can't control it.'

She moaned deep in her throat as his mouth brushed satin-smooth skin in tiny, burning kisses as he moved the lace covering of her nightie under her breasts and explored their softness.

'I could have killed Donnie for looking at you the way he did,' he said huskily after a long moment, when he raised his head to look into her drowning violet eyes. 'Do you know that? I've never felt like that in my life.'

Because he'd never had anyone deny him what he wanted before? she asked herself painfully as she desperately tried to keep a hold on reality. It couldn't be anything more than that; he had told her so himself. And forbidden fruit was always sweeter; everyone knew that.

But then he took her mouth again, moulding her into the hard-muscled planes of his chest as he pulled her fiercely against him, and logic flew out of the window. Her eyes shut, she abandoned herself to the sweetness of the moment, his lips moving with devastating experience and hot sensuality over her eyes, her mouth and down to her throat and breasts, leaving a trail of fire and sensuous delight wherever they touched. She needed him, she wanted him, but most of all she loved him, and she knew that she would never love any man but Reece.

Surely it wouldn't be wrong to take what he offered, even if it had to last her a lifetime? And it might work. He might just find that when the time came to let her go he couldn't—mightn't he?

The answer came coldly and steadily from somewhere deep within that still remained hers. He might give her the physical gift of his body for a few weeks, a few months, but that would be all. And it wouldn't be enough.

She pulled away from him abruptly, her body freezing. If he couldn't love her it would be like having the most wonderful present in the world wrapped up in shiny, glittering paper but with the proviso that it must never be unwrapped, never be enjoyed. A gift that was no gift at all.

'Please leave, Reece.'

'Leave?' He had taken a step back as she had jerked away, his eyes narrowing like twin blades on her face. 'Are you sure that's what you want?' He was asking about more than just the immediate moment and she knew it.

'Yes.' She raised her head carefully, her face white. 'I'm quite sure.'

And after he'd gone, banging the door behind him with unnecessary force, she realised that for the first time since she had met him she *was* sure. She had just sentenced herself to misery and loneliness, to a life that even now gripped her with panic, but she was still sure that it was the only way to go. It was over, finished, done with. Now all she had to do was learn to live with the annihilation of all her dreams and hopes.

CHAPTER NINE

THE next morning, after a few hours' troubled sleep, Miriam arose to find that nature had conspired to set Barbara's wedding day in a morning of exquisite winter beauty. As she glanced out of the window just before five the still, white world outside was transparently ethereal, the thick snow scattered with a million glittering crystals from the harsh frost during the night and the trees and bushes silent and motionless in the hushed, cold air.

The serene tranquillity was like a balm to her sore heart as she forced herself to eat a slice of toast and drink a cup of coffee before starting work, and when the others arrived, along with the extra staff they had taken on for the day, the sheer pace of work drove everything but the success of the next few hours out of her mind.

She had promised Barbara a few days before that she would try and make the church for the actual ceremony, and was more than a little touched when Barbara swept into the kitchens at just after nine to remind her of the fact.

'You look lovely, just lovely.' She hastily ushered Reece's sister out of the chaos in the kitchen, fearing for her dress, and into the big hall where most of the family were assembling, awaiting the fleet of cars that were to take them to the church. Craig had already left an hour or so earlier with Donnie, his best man, on Barbara's explicit instructions. She had been terrified he would see her before the ceremony, convinced it was bad luck.

'Do you think so?' Barbara's face was pale under the carefully applied make-up, her eyes anxious. 'Miriam, he's so much younger than me. What if he has second thoughts, or takes one look at me and bolts?'

'Don't be so ridiculous.' Miriam was going to smile, thinking that Barbara was half-joking, but then she saw the tremulous mouth and fear in the lovely grey eyes. 'You look beautiful, Barbara, absolutely beautiful, but even if you didn't it wouldn't make any difference to Craig.' She stepped back a pace to admire the calf-length, wildly expensive, crushed silk dress in pale apricot, with its tiny matching hat and veil. 'He loves you; you're the only one for him, so just enjoy the day.'

'Good advice.' She forced herself to show no reaction whatsoever as Reece's deep voice sounded over her shoulder, and counted to ten before she nerved herself to turn and face him. He looked wonderful—she had known that he would—resplendent in top hat and tails in smoky grey, the cut of the material accentuating his broad shoulders and muscled frame and causing the breath to catch in her throat. 'Barbara tells me you're coming to the church,' he said quietly as his eyes wandered over her flushed face and tousled hair. 'Is that right?'

'Yes.' She was instantly on the defensive. 'I'm going to change in just a minute,' she added quickly, suspecting that he disapproved of the casual trousers and blouse that she was wearing.

'I was just going to say there are several trays of buttonholes in the hall if you would like to help yourself to one as you leave,' he answered mildly, before turning away to speak to one of Craig's numerous relations and leaving her to give her best wishes to Barbara.

She hurried back to the kitchens to explain that she was slipping away for an hour, only to get embroiled in one panic after another. The church service was at ten and the family left at half past nine, at which point she fled into the flat and threw the dress and coat she had put by for the morning onto her hot, sticky frame.

Both Barbara and Reece had insisted that she could use Barbara's neat little sports car over the weekend, but after last night she couldn't bring herself to drive it and trundled off to the church a few miles away in the large van that Mitch had driven that morning. There were no parking spaces within a hundred-yard radius of the church and she had just emerged from the van, hot and flustered after persuading it into a space that just fitted, when a coolly amused female voice sounded just behind her.

'Hello again...' She turned slowly, her instinct rather than her ears telling her whom the voice belonged to. Sharon was standing to one side of an imperious Mercedes which her parents were just leaving, her silver blonde hair coiled into an elegant chignon on which a tiny little green hat nestled, her tall, slim body clothed in an exquisitely cut, close-fitting green suit of the same hue, enhancing the big emerald eyes into dark pools. 'Miriam, isn't it?'

'Yes. Good morning.' As she spoke she smiled and nodded at Sharon's parents, who inclined their heads coldly, their faces plainly stating that they found it extraordinary that their precious daughter was talking to someone who had just emerged from a somewhat dirty old van.

'You're going to the church?' Sharon's voice held just the right note of surprised disapproval, and as the chilly gaze moved slowly, and pointedly, over Miriam's clothes Miriam's chin rose a few notches in answer to the unspoken insult. 'I mean, you must have masses to do,' Sharon drawled sweetly as she began to walk away, linking her arm in that of her father's.

There had been no need of a reply, and as Miriam locked the van's door she found that she was grinding her teeth together in impotent rage. It doesn't matter— *she* doesn't matter, she told herself firmly as she followed quickly in the Berkely-Smiths' footsteps, fearing she would be late. She was just behind them as they began to walk up the long, winding path to the church door and quite able to hear their conversation, spoken as it was in a loud, cultured drawl. 'But, darling,' Sharon's mother was saying as her ridiculously flowered hat bobbed precariously on the back of her obviously dyed chestnut hair, 'what would give the girl the idea she could come to the wedding if she's just one of the caterers?'

'I don't know.' Sharon's voice was irritated and tight. 'But that is exactly what she is, I can assure you. One of Reece's temporary employees. But you know how some of these people are, Mummy...' And somehow, instantly, Miriam knew that Sharon was aware of her just behind them. 'Give them an inch and they take a mile. Reece was complaining about it only the other day.'

'Well, something ought to be done...'

As they disappeared into the small, arched porch of the old medieval church Miriam stood stock-still on the path, her heart pounding with the shock of the bitterly barbed words. How could people be like that? She stared after them into the shadowed porch beyond which the lighted church glowed brightly. So spiteful, so malicious?

She glanced down at her best coat, which had cost her far more than she had been able to afford a few months before. OK, so it wasn't an exclusive with a four-number price-tag, but it wasn't exactly a bit of rag either.

She shut her eyes tightly and then set her mouth in a grim line as hot rage replaced the hurt and surprise. And she didn't believe for a moment that Reece would have discussed her with Sharon, although that was what the blonde girl had been insinuating. He wouldn't. He just wouldn't. Would he? She bit her lip hard and then gathered all her courage around her as she marched into the cold church.

'Bride or groom?' A young, bright-eyed usher was at her side instantly as he handed her an order of service.

'Bride.' Once seated between an elderly couple on her right, who smelt of lavender and country cottages, and a cool-eyed businesswoman on her left, who she just knew was a lawyer friend of Barbara's, Miriam took stock. She would wait until Barbara had arrived and then slip quietly out of the church at some point during the service; seated as she was at the back of the church, it would be no problem. And she *wasn't* running away. She quelled the little voice in the back of her mind with fierce determination. She needed to get back to the house; she had a million things to do, that was all.

As the Bridal March brought a hushed silence to the subdued chattering she took a deep breath and composed herself, her glance drawn helplessly to Reece as he escorted his sister down the aisle. She couldn't bear this; she really couldn't.

As she glanced through the throng to his tall, straight figure in sombre grey, Barbara like a lovely bird of paradise on his arm, she bit back the tears with superhuman effort. Would he ever marry? She saw the back of his head through a mist of emotion as they continued to the front of the flower-bedecked church. And if so what would she be like? A contained, cucumber-cool blonde? A sultry brunette? Or maybe a redhead like herself? And would the future Mrs Vance know that he didn't love her, that he thought himself incapable of love, or would she be able to penetrate that hard outer shell to the real man within, whom she herself had glimpsed once or twice?

She looked down as the minister began to speak, searching her bag for a tissue and wiping her eyes carefully. It was all right. Everyone cried at weddings. As the service continued she fought for control.

And then, almost against her will, her glance was drawn once more to the front of the church as she searched him out. She saw his dark head instantly, and also the blonde-haired one beside it, complete with little green hat, and Sharon's parents cosily seated in the pew directly behind them. The perfect family picture, in fact, and one of undeniable intent in the circumstances?

Even as she watched, Sharon whispered something in Reece's ear, her profile strikingly lovely even at that distance, and as Reece bent to listen Miriam saw Sharon deposit a swift kiss on his smooth, tanned cheek.

Well, what had she expected? She closed her eyes, wishing that she were anywhere but in this church at this precise moment. For Sharon to leave her parents and join him in the front row meant far, far more than mere seating arrangements. As the choir led the congregation in the first hymn she slipped out silently into the cold white world outside, her mind and emotions going into a deep freeze as icy as the air around her.

By twelve o'clock midday everything was ready for the expected guests and bridal party, and as Miriam and Mitch took a few minutes out to enjoy a quiet cup of coffee in the flat away from the others Miriam caught her brother looking at her with a distinctly worried gleam in his eye. 'OK,' he said flatly, after a few minutes of total silence. 'Let's have it; what's wrong?'

'Wrong?' She forced a brittle smile. 'I don't know what you mean.'

'It's him, isn't it?' Mitch eyed her grimly. 'I knew it. Has he made a pass or something?'

'Mitch, I really don't think—'

'You haven't said a word in five minutes, which is a record for you,' Mitch said quietly. 'Now, I'm your brother, Mim, and I love you. At the very least you could give me a clue about what's going on.'

She opened her mouth to deny everything but instead found herself confiding in Mitch in a way she hadn't done since they were children. 'So that's it,' she said flatly as she came to the end of the monologue. 'End of story. Not that there ever was one really.'

Mitch swore a particularly virulent oath that made her wince as her eyes fastened on his angry face. 'I knew I should have taken this job.'

'I wish you had.' The ice encasing her heart had begun to melt as she had spoken, and for the first time since seeing Reece and Sharon together in the church hot anger began to seep into the crevices.

From the very beginning Reece had thought that he could dictate all the rules, she thought furiously, even going so far as to set them out in cold, clinical detail before she had even said that she was interested. The sheer ego of the man! And the self-obsession. However he dressed it up, he had warned her of the consequences of getting involved with him while making play after play for her, and all the while sweet little Sharon had been there in the background for when he tired of the game. Well, enough was enough.

She turned to Mitch, who had been watching the play of emotions across her expressive face with both apprehension and interest. 'But you didn't,' she continued tightly, 'and we've got a job to do, and then we can get the hell out of here and never have to speak to Reece Vance again.'

'Will you?' Mitch caught her arm as she stood up. 'Leave and shake the dust off, so to speak?'

'I already have.' She gazed at him for a long moment and then walked back to the kitchens, her back straight. She would get through the rest of this day with her head held high and then pick up the pieces of her shattered heart later. She'd have all the time in the world, after all.

Once the guests arrived the rest of the afternoon became a blur of frenzied activity. Barbara came straight to the kitchens to seek Miriam out, her lovely face radiant. 'I want you to have this.' She placed her wedding bouquet of white and apricot roses into Miriam's arms. 'I didn't throw it,' she added unnecessarily, 'although Sharon was hovering like some demented bluebottle.'

At the sound of the other woman's name the tears that had threatened to fall at Barbara's kindness dried instantly. 'It's beautiful.' Miriam bent and sniffed the softly curled blooms. 'And it smells wonderful.'

'You've made my day, Miriam.' Barbara's eyes were full of happy, sparkling tears, but strangely Miriam suddenly felt as though she would never be able to cry again in the whole of her life. 'You've worked so hard.'

'It's my job.' She softened the words with a smile and a hug, but as Barbara left to join the guests in the big hall she stared after her expressionlessly. That was all it was—a job. *Just a job.* Suddenly the difference between Reece's world and her own had never been greater.

The buffet was kept well-stocked all day, and with four waiters to ensure that no one had an empty glass the merriment was high by evening. She avoided Reece all afternoon, which wasn't too difficult—Sharon was attached like a limpet to his arm, and if Miriam hadn't known better she would have sworn that the elegant blonde was the hostess as she smiled and chatted with gracious composure at his side.

Miriam was just replacing an empty tray of cold meats with a full one when she felt a cool tap on her shoulder and turned to look straight into hard green eyes a few inches away from her own. 'Still working like a little beaver?' Sharon laughed patronisingly. 'It makes me absolutely exhausted just to watch you attending to all our needs.'

'Does it?' Steady, Miriam, steady, she warned herself as a whole host of hot words sprang onto her tongue. If Sharon wanted to cast herself in the role of lady of the manor then that was up to her—and Reece. She only had to stand the other woman a few more hours after all, and she just wasn't worth jeopardising their reference for. 'Well, an event like this doesn't just run itself,'

Miriam said coolly, her face straight. 'It takes a lot of planning and a great deal of hard work.'

'Oh, I can see that.' Sharon's barracuda-type smile faded as she slanted her lovely green eyes to accompany a disdainful pout. 'But don't you find it all so boring? I'd just die if I had to cook all day; I'm afraid I can't boil an egg.'

'Really?' Miriam signalled for Vera to take some dirty plates into the kitchen. 'Well, neither can Barbara, so you're in good company,' she said politely as she tried to edge away.

'But Barbara's got Craig now, and I understand he's divine in the kitchen,' Sharon drawled slowly. 'What Reece and I shall do heaven only knows; thank goodness for Mrs Goode.' She smiled coldly. 'We shall have to take her with us when we holiday abroad.'

The message was clear and Miriam knew that her shock had registered on her face as the other woman's smile widened with satisfaction.

'But we'll remember your little firm for the reception, sweetie...' Sharon tapped her arm condescendingly. 'Good workers are *so* hard to find these days. Reece often complains about that very thing; he's such an old crosspatch at times but I can usually find some way to... console him.'

'You'll have to excuse me.' Miriam looked straight into the lovely face, not bothering to try and hide her disdain for the innuendo and double talk as her lip curled slightly. 'This particular worker has things to do.'

She walked away steadily, her back straight and her head high, but once in the outside corridor she turned into the privacy of the flat, collapsing with her back against the door as she fought silently for control. So they were lovers? So what was new? She had known, hadn't she? And the reference to their marriage, the sly insinuation about the reception...?

'I don't believe it...' She heard her whisper in the empty room with a sudden surge of self-contempt. What did it matter what she believed? Reece certainly didn't care one way or the other, and she was blowed if she was going to skulk in here like a small, frightened rabbit. She would do what she had determined to do—get through this day and then go on from there, although where to she didn't have a clue.

She drew a deep breath, brushed back a few wisps of hair that had come adrift from the tidy pony-tail at the back of her head, and smoothed down the neat blue dress that they had decided on as a uniform for the female staff when a function was on. There was a strange sour taste in her mouth and a dead weight where her heart should have been but she was damned if she would ever let him know how much he had hurt her. She'd get through this with some dignity if it killed her.

She pulled open the door and stepped smartly into the corridor outside, only to bump headlong into Donnie, who looked as though he was loitering outside.

'Oh, hi.' The friendly grin was the last thing she needed at this moment, she thought helplessly as she forced her frozen mouth to respond in kind. 'I've been looking for you,' he said quickly. 'You've been like a will-o'-the-wisp today—here one minute and gone the next.'

'Lost, Donnie?' The cool, deep voice from the end doorway brought both their heads jerking round, and Miriam saw that Reece's face was cold and expressionless as he stared their way, leaning lazily against the open doorway as the silver eyes flicked tightly over Donnie's startled face.

'Not exactly.' Craig's brother laughed nervously as he moved away from Miriam. 'Just wanted a word with this little lady, here.'

'I'd rather you didn't.' Now the dark voice was positively icy. 'This is Barbara's big day and I've paid a fortune to have the caterers catering; know what I mean?'

It was insulting, both to her and the big Australian, and
she saw Donnie stiffen slightly as his eyes evaluated
Reece's powerful frame and massive shoulders before he
seemed to concede defeat.

'No problem.' He smiled again but it didn't reach the
blue eyes. 'I'll go and grab myself another beer; that's
one thing I do like about this freezing-cold country—
the beer.'

Reece didn't reply verbally or by so much as the flicker
of an eyelash, and after another long, embarrassing
moment Donnie sauntered towards him, edging past
without looking at him and entering the noise beyond.

'That was incredibly rude.' She faced him angrily, her
cheeks glowing bright scarlet and her eyes flashing.
'There was absolutely no need to behave like that.'

'This is my house, Miriam; I behave exactly as I want
to,' he said icily. 'Now, can you organise your people to
start clearing away, please? I intend to have the fireworks in an hour or so, and after that the fruit and
champagne, of course. Keep your mind on what you are
being paid to do rather than flirting with my guests.'

He shut the door before she had a chance to reply,
which was just as well because even she didn't know that
she knew some of the words she muttered furiously after
him.

The fireworks went off without a hitch, lighting up the
dark sky with glittering stars and curls to the ac-
companiment of oohs and aahs by the assembled guests
and shrill squeals from the children who were present.
The strawberries were consumed with every appearance
of enjoyment, the excellent champagne drunk with relish,
and back in the kitchen, as the staff brought the last
dishes through, Mitch suddenly grabbed her and swung
her round, his voice exuberant.

'Perfect. You planned it all perfectly, Mim.' He released her, to stand grinning down into her exhausted

face. 'And we pulled it off, didn't we? I had my doubts whether we ever would.'

'Did you?' She forced a smile from somewhere and then sat down rather suddenly on a chair.

'You're whacked.' Mitch waved a hand at the chaos behind them. 'We'll see to all this; you go to bed.'

'No.' There was still far too much to do. 'But I think I'll go and get a breath of fresh air if you don't mind. I won't be long.' She had to do something to combat this faintness she was feeling.

'Be as long as you like,' Mitch said cheerfully. 'I think our reference is guaranteed now, don't you?'

Damn the reference. As she fetched her coat from the flat and walked through to the garden from the door at the end of the corridor she was conscious that she was feeling most unlike herself. She couldn't have named the emotions that were bubbling away deep in her chest to anyone, but a burning rage was there, as well as crucifying hurt and pain, and as the icy cold air hit her hot face she took a long, deep gasp of its crystal cleanness, shutting her eyes for a moment then opening them to walk quietly round to the side of the house that was not overlooked by any windows.

The night was deathly quiet and still, the sky a dark blanket in which a million twinkling stars provided a natural display that was more impressive than any man-made explosions and coloured sparks, and already frost was thick on the top of the snow, its glittering crystals picked out by the moonlight that was flooding the pale winter night.

Her feet were wet through within seconds, and too late she remembered that she had forgotten to change her light working shoes, but it didn't matter. She leant against the trunk of a silver birch and shut her eyes tightly. Nothing mattered. She was way, way out of her league with this thing, and the only person she could blame was herself.

She couldn't even blame Reece—she felt the urge to howl and scream take hold and bit it back savagely—not really, not if she was honest. *He* had been brutally honest all along in making it plain that the only emotion he could feel for her was one of male sexual desire. Probably that was all he felt for Sharon too, but the difference was that she was like him, she could cope with how he was—enjoy it, even. Miriam shook her head silently. And soon he would be out of her life for good. It was too much to take in.

She heard the footsteps behind her just a second too late to turn as a pair of hard and very strong male arms enclosed her from behind, hugging her to a broad chest at the same time as a prickly face nuzzled into her neck. For a second, just a second, she thought it might be Reece, and then Donnie's Australian twang destroyed what she was forced to acknowledge had been—crazily—hope.

'I've been waiting to do this all day.' His breath smelt strongly of beer and his voice was slurred—two facts that she absorbed at the same time as she felt his hands move up and under her coat, fastening on her breasts with supreme disregard for any niceties.

'Stop it.' She jerked in his hold as she slapped at his hands, but it had the same effect as hitting out at a block of granite.

'Aw, c'mon, Miriam, relax a little,' he said thickly as he turned her round within his arms. 'There's no one around—'

'Wrong.' Reece's voice was like a pistol shot in the cold air, and Miriam nearly jumped out of her skin as Donnie jerked violently with surprise. The next moment he had been plucked away, to be thrown to one side so savagely that he lost his footing and sprawled helplessly in the snow, a large lilac bush depositing its mantle of thick snow on the top of him as he banged into its trunk. 'The good time is *in* the house,' Reece growled grimly as the fair-haired man struggled to his feet, swearing profusely, 'and cut the bad language.'

'Like hell I will!' As Donnie made a swing for his jaw Reece moved slightly to one side, trapping the other man's arm behind his back as he forced him to his knees.

'You're way out of line here, mister,' he breathed tightly as he bent over Donnie's groaning form. 'Now, we can play this the nice way and assume you've had a bit too much to drink and are very sorry for bothering this young lady, or we can take matters further and see which of us ends up in the hospital first—'

'Please stop.' Miriam sprang in front of them both, her voice shrill and frightened. 'You're going to ruin Barbara's and Craig's wedding day if you fight. Please, just leave it.'

'Well?' Reece stepped back a pace as he let go of Donnie's arm, and the big man raised himself to his feet, his face red and scowling. 'Are you going to listen to good advice?'

'I don't know what all the fuss is about.' Donnie shook his head as his words blurred and ran into each other again. 'I wasn't going to rape her; I only wanted—'

'We both know what you wanted and it's no go.' Reece looked as though he was prepared to do murder, and after another sidelong glance at his dark, angry face Donnie clearly felt that discretion was the better part of valour as he brushed himself down, muttering quietly under his breath before turning and walking away.

Miriam watched him go until he disappeared from view into the house, her hands pressed in fists against her cheeks, and then she turned to Reece to see him watching her through deadly cold, narrowed eyes. 'Satisfied?' he asked tightly.

'Satisfied?' She stared at him as shock and relief warred with surprise. 'I don't know what you mean.'

'Don't give me that.' The silver gaze was lethal. 'Are you telling me you didn't arrange to meet that lout out here? You must have known what to expect.'

'I'm not telling you anything,' she snapped back furiously. 'As usual, it's you making all the assumptions.' She couldn't believe that he was acting this way, not with his present mistress and soon-to-be wife, who hadn't left his side all day, established cosily in the house and no doubt awaiting his return with eager anticipation.

'It doesn't need a great mathematician to put two and two together,' he growled tightly.

'And in this case come up with an answer of ten.' She drew her coat more closely around her as the cold began to make her feet numb. 'I don't have to explain myself to you and I have no intention of doing so,' she stated flatly. 'Now, I'm sure Sharon's waiting for you so if you've quite finished—'

'Damn Sharon.' He caught hold of her arm as he pulled her sharply to face him. 'And you're wrong; you do have to explain such conduct to me. In case you've forgotten, you are here for the express purpose of carrying out a job for me—'

'*I know!*' She was aware that her control had gone, totally, but she didn't care. The culmination of weeks and days and hours of being on a constant knife-edge, combined with the bitter hurt and humiliation that she had suffered that day at his hands, caused an explosion that nothing and no one could have prevented. 'Oh, believe me, I know; I've had it shoved down my throat enough today never to forget it.'

'Meaning?'

'Meaning whatever you like.' She glared at him, jerking his hand off her arm and baring her teeth like a small, cornered animal. 'Now just leave me alone, Reece, and get back to the people who matter.' One in particular.

'And I was beginning to think you just might be different.' His laugh was harsh and caustic in the biting air. 'But you're just the same as all the others after all.'

'The others?' Funnily enough, his words caused an ice-cold anger that was more potent than any hysterical rage. 'And you'd know plenty about *others* wouldn't you, Reece?' she said bitterly. 'Well, I'm sorry, Mr Iceman. I'm sure it would be convenient for you to package me up and slot me into one of the holes in that tidy little mind of yours but I won't oblige.' She was shaking from head to foot, but more with fury than cold. 'I'm not going to fit into your concept of what a female should be like, any more than I'm going to excuse your spineless attitude to life and love.'

'Spineless?' For a moment she thought that he was going to hit her so great was his rage, but she didn't move an inch, her eyes burning with hot tears that she was determined he would never see.

'Yes, spineless,' she reiterated tightly. 'What else would you call it when you try to get me into bed at the same time as telling me that it will only be a light affair, that you'll never love me or be prepared to stay? You were making excuses for yourself in advance, preparing an escape route just in case you should start to feel something for me and panic, and then you could turn round with the immortal line of "I told you so".'

'It wasn't like that—'

'Yes, it was.' She backed from him now, her face scarlet. '*It was*. I hate you. I hate this place and your life and everything about you. I wish I'd never met you. You deserve people like Sharon—that's the truth of it. You wouldn't know a real woman if one rose up and bit you! You're shallow, that's all. Shallow and cold and I must have been mad to think I was in love with you.'

He stood completely motionless, a grey stone statue in the darkness, as she turned and ran for the house, sobbing helplessly as the realisation of what she had just said and done washed over her in a searing flood. She went straight to the flat, locking the door behind her and throwing herself on the carpet as she cried as though her heart would break—long, shuddering sobs that tore from her body in pain and despair and confusion.

How could she have said all that? she asked herself weakly after long minutes as she curled into a tight little ball. He would never forgive her, never. If there had been the slightest hope for the future—anything—she had just destroyed it more effectively than Sharon could ever have done.

It was a good deal later that she heard the knock on the door, and as she froze, her hand going to her mouth as her breathing stopped, the relief was indescribable as Mitch's voice sounded outside. 'Mim? Are you in there?'

Once he was in the tears started again, but this time there was none of the tearing anguish of before, just a numb, empty hopelessness that seemed to fill her body and mind until she felt as though she was in a black void where nothing good could ever penetrate again. 'I want to go home, Mitch.' She raised her head as her brother came in with the coffee that he had insisted on making. 'I've had enough.'

'You're exhausted.' He patted her arm ineffectually. She hadn't told him what had transpired, beyond a brief outline of Donnie's advances and the way Reece had dealt with him. 'Things never get you down normally; you need a break.'

He sat down opposite her on one of the easy chairs. 'I'll stay here tonight and oversee everything. There won't be too much to do tomorrow, so why don't you take some time off and get away? You've worked damn hard on this one, Mim, and worn yourself to a frazzle. We've nothing heavy for the next few weeks, and with the amount we're getting for this job, and our order book for next year, we've got no problems financially. Why don't you disappear for three or four weeks in the sun?

You haven't had a holiday for years and it'd do you good.'

'I might just do that.' She smiled weakly and forced herself to accept the coffee and drink it as though her world hadn't just fallen apart. 'If you're sure you can cope.'

'Sure I'm sure.' Mitch grinned and walked into the bedroom, packing her case and bringing it through to the lounge. 'Now, I'll sleep here tonight and clear things tomorrow. You go home and take the phone off the hook and get some rest. Come on.' He took her arm, pulling her to her feet and picking up the case with his other hand. 'The car's outside; I came in it this morning. You use that as the vans are both here too.'

She could never remember driving home that night, the next few hours blurring for ever in her mind, but when she awoke the next morning to a Sunday filled with bright winter sunshine something had clarified in her mind during the long night hours. She was eaten up with misery and jealousy and anger and she didn't like herself like this—she didn't like it at all. Some of what she had screamed at Reece the night before had been the truth and some of it had been a result of her blinding jealousy and hurt, but whatever, it couldn't continue.

She took a long, deep breath as she lay in the snug warmth of her bed watching a dancing ray of white sunlight on the far wall. Mitch was right; she had to get away and try and get herself together. She couldn't go on like this. She didn't want to. She wanted to be able at least to like herself again, even if she wasn't someone that Reece Vance could love.

CHAPTER TEN

MITCH banked the enormous cheque that Reece had given him on Sunday prompt and early Monday morning, and before Miriam left for Morocco later that day she wrote another cheque to cover the whole of the debt outstanding on the vans, along with a formal little note of thanks expressing best wishes for himself and Sharon in their future together.

It nearly killed her to do it but, once done, the solid weight that had settled where her heart should have been was a little easier. If she could do this she could do anything, she thought wryly as she watched the buff coloured envelope slip into the postbox with a dull thud.

And later that afternoon, as she sat in the airport departure lounge on the first stage of her month's holiday to Morocco, which she had got at a ridiculously low price due to a last-minute cancellation by the original ticket holders, she reflected flatly that she had learnt more about herself in the last few weeks than in the whole of all the years before.

She had never imagined spending Christmas alone in a foreign country for a start, but the date of the holiday was such that she would be travelling home at the beginning of the new year and it amazed her that she didn't even care. She had written no Christmas cards, bought no presents, would be detached from the last-minute rush involving Christmas trees, turkeys and plum puddings and all she could feel was indifference.

What have you done to me, Reece? she asked herself more than once on the uneventful plane journey. Would

he joy of living ever revive? It frightened her that she
didn't know and didn't care.

he spent the first few days in Casablanca by the hotel
pool, reading, sleeping and eating. She felt strange when
he stopped to analyse it, almost as though she were
onvalescing after a serious illness that had taken every
scrap of energy and drive and left her an empty, damaged
hell.

And she was still feeling exactly the same on the fol-
owing Tuesday, when she had been in Morocco just over
a week. She had visited one or two mosques, their
owering minarets and beautiful arches delicate and
imeless under the hot Eastern sun, and wandered slowly
n the countless souks—markets filled with tiny stalls
where, in the ancient way of Eastern peoples, merchants
haggled over the prices with their customers. And
lthough England with its snow and winter chill seemed
million miles away still the feeling of unreality persisted.

So, as she opened sleep-filled eyes after dozing lazily
n a comfortable sun-lounger at the edge of the pool
or most of the afternoon, the fact that Reece was lying
ot three feet away from her took a second or two to
ink in.

She stared at him mindlessly and the beautiful silver-
rey eyes stared back, his black hair gleaming in the last
f the dying sunlight and his big body naked except for
pair of brief swimming trunks.

'Hello, Miriam.' It was his voice that convinced her
t wasn't a dream—that deep, dark voice that had made
er mad on occasion with its cool, authoritative tone
nd arrogant self-assurance.

'I—' She struggled into a sitting position as she became
ware of two things simultaneously. One was the fact
hat the brief bikini that she was wearing left very little
o the imagination, and the other, intrinsically linked

with the first, was the effect that the sight of his near naked body was having on hers.

He looked magnificent but she had known he would she thought desperately as her brain began to function again. 'Where's Sharon?' She glanced round her helplessly, as though the lovely blonde was going to drop out of the sky like the wicked witch of the East.

'Sharon?' His eyes narrowed slightly, but apart from that he didn't move a muscle. 'I've no idea. Should I have?'

'But—' She stopped abruptly again and then, mercifully, hot rage began to sweep away the confusion and panic and loosen her tongue. 'Of course you should,' she said tightly as she reached down by the side of the lounger for her robe and moved her feet over the side of the plastic frame as she slipped it on.

The rush of love and longing that had deluged her since she had opened her eyes had to be brought under control, she told herself desperately as she kept her face in profile to the piercing gaze. He mustn't guess—

'Why?' He was leaning on one elbow as he watched her, the epitome of the relaxed holiday-maker, and for a moment she could have kicked him for that casual confidence.

'Look, I don't know why you're here but—'

'I'm here to see you, Miriam, and, for the record, couldn't care less where Sharon is now or at any other time,' he said quietly, bringing her eyes to his with a little snap. 'I don't know what that lady has been telling you—'

'She's been *telling* me about your plans for the future,' Miriam said tightly, 'which I suppose you are now going to deny?' She laughed harshly, the sound jarring in the thick, scented air and causing the one or two hotel guests who were left by the pool to glance over before returning to their magazines. 'As if you could.'

'I could.' He sat up now, swinging his feet over the side of his lounger and taking her arm in his. 'Put your sandals on,' he said grimly. 'We're going for a walk in the gardens.'

'I'm not going anywhere with you—'

'You damn well are.' He cut short her outraged protest with an intimidatingly firm voice as he reached down for his shirt and forced her upwards. 'And if you object I'll carry you if necessary. We're going to talk somewhere private, and as you'd probably throw a blue fit if I suggested my room or yours the gardens will have to do.'

She opened her mouth to protest further, but the look in the narrowed grey eyes convinced her that he meant exactly what he said, and she couldn't face the sort of scene that would follow if she refused. She pulled the belt of her robe angrily tight, knotting it firmly round her waist—a gesture that wasn't lost on Reece and which caused his hard mouth to straighten further as he led her away from the pool to the rambling, ornate gardens that surrounded the hotel, full of small, secluded bowers and wooden seats with the odd sparkling fountain here and there.

She was trembling violently and to her chagrin knew that he must be able to feel it through his hand on her arm, but there was nothing she could do but brazen it out, humiliating though it was. She raised her chin defiantly as her thoughts went into hyper-drive.

Why was he here? Her heart thudded painfully as the thought that had tormented her for days came to the forefront of her mind. She had told him that she was in love with him in the last heated seconds of that awful row. She blinked as her skin burnt with embarrassment. How could she have done the one thing that she had purposed not to? But it was too late now. Was that why he was here? To capitalise on what he would almost cer-

tainly see as a weakness? But how had he found ou
where to find her?

'Mitch told me you were here.' It was almost as thoug
he had read her mind. 'After a little persuading,' h
added grimly.

'You didn't hurt him?' she asked weakly, suddenl
horrified as the thought occurred.

'Of course I didn't hurt him; he's your brother, fc
crying out loud!' Reece glared at her in amazemer
before stopping at a quiet, secluded bench set back in
small half-circle of bushes and forcing her down on th
sun-warmed wood. 'I just meant that it took me som
time, that's all—a week, in fact. He was determined nc
to give away your hidey-hole—'

'It's not a hidey-hole.' She reared up like a scalde
cat, her cheeks scarlet with humiliation and rage. 'I cam
away for a few days in the sun, that's all.'

'Well, I sure as hell didn't.' He sat down beside he
and she tried to block the smell and nearness of hir
from her senses as her body reacted with a million littl
signals sending shivers all down her limbs. His shirt wa
undone, his dark, hair-roughened chest and muscle
frame in full view, and she had never, ever thought t
feel as she was feeling now about a man's body. Sh
knew that the male of the species was prone to uncor
trollable urges, but the female?

'We need to talk, Miriam.' He turned slightly, one ar
along the back of the seat as he watched her trouble
profile. 'And the first thing is that I am not involve
with Sharon in any way—never have been and never wi
be. She is a friend, or more precisely the daughter c
my parents' friends, and that's all. Due to the close r
lationship between the two sets of parents she has alway
been around and, as Barbara reminded me most forcibl
before she went off on honeymoon, prone to take ou
rageous advantage given half a chance, but I have neve
found her in the slightest bit attractive. That's the truth

He gestured irritably with one hand. 'She is far too like her mother for a start.'

'But—' She stared at him with huge, wide eyes. 'But?'

'She said you were going to get married, that you were already... close,' Miriam whispered painfully.

'Like I said, she is a carbon copy of her mother who is a twin spirit to my mother,' he stated grimly, his mouth tight. 'I could strangle the lot of them.'

'Is that why you're here?' she asked faintly, her face confused. 'Just to tell me you aren't having an affair with Sharon?'

'No.' He had turned away, but now swung to face her again, raising tortured eyes to hers. 'I'm going mad, Miriam...' He raked his hair back savagely. 'Stark, staring mad—but I have to ask. Did you mean it?'

'What?' She knew what he meant but couldn't reply as she gazed into the silver-grey eyes that were suddenly anything but cold and distant. That look in his eyes—it couldn't be what she thought it was. She was imagining things again, things born out of her desperate love for him.

'When you said—' He took a deep, hard pull of air and she realised, with a throb of incredulity, that he was nervous. 'When you said you had thought you were in love with me,' he said gruffly.

'I—' The words strangled and died in her throat. She couldn't—she just couldn't open herself to more humiliation and pain. What did he want with her, for goodness' sake? Hadn't he hurt her enough?

'Listen to me,' he whispered huskily, and her eyes opened wide in shock at the sound of his voice. She had never thought to hear the great and invincible Reece Vance plead, but she was hearing it now. 'Just listen, and then at the end of it if you want me to go, if it's all too late, I'll clear out of this hotel and your life for ever.'

'Reece—'

'Since the day I met you I've been in the worst so
of hell you could imagine,' he said softly, his voice u.
steady and full of pain. 'Everything about you, eve
little thing I loved—' He shook his head as he stoppe
abruptly. 'I don't mean just your looks, although the
are perfect, but the whole of you. Your honesty, th
devastating frankness, the natural gaiety and warmth th
draws people like moths to a flame—it's been crucifyi
me hour by hour, Miriam.'

'But why?' Her face was white with shock and b
wilderment even as the hope that she had thought de:
began to smoulder in the ashes.

'Because you were right, that night of Barbara
wedding,' he said grimly as he stood up to stand wi
his back towards her and watch the glittering play
water in the small fountain. 'You called me spineles:
accused me of all manner of crimes and you were rig
in most of them. I was terrified to trust my heart whe
you were concerned. I've never been in love before—
hell, I didn't even believe in the damn concept—and a
of a sudden the thing hits me like a ton of bricks ar
I'm out for the count.

'You said, when you were fighting so vehemently f
Barbara's happiness, that she is the type of person wh
only loves once, and when I heard it it was like a thu:
derbolt straight through my heart. I knew it—deep insi
I knew it. Because I'm the same. I'd already fallen
love with you but I couldn't let myself believe it. Dammi
my own sister had more guts than me!'

He began to pace in front of her as she sat in stunne
silence, not daring to move.

'Those apes Gregory sent round that day—I could ha
cheerfully wiped them from the face of the earth f
daring to frighten you the way they did, with their threa
and bullying. I wanted to protect you, take care of yo
cherish you—' He groaned out loud as he drove or
hand into his fist. 'Yes, and love and adore you. All th

things my father felt for my mother, that nearly destroyed him and ruined his peace of mind from the day he met her.'

'But your mother didn't love your father or anyone,' she whispered through numb lips. 'You told me that—'

'And you didn't love me.' He stopped to face her, his eyes agonised. 'Hell, you didn't even like me. There was just this physical attraction, that was all. It was so damn ironic—' He shook his head savagely.

'But you had told me you would never love me,' she said softly as her heart began to beat so fast that she thought she would faint. 'You said all you could ever offer was a brief affair—'

'I lied.' He laughed harshly—a dry, raw sound that made her flinch. 'To myself as much as you. You'd turned my world upside down and I was desperately trying to right it in the only way I knew how.'

Oh, Reece, Reece, Reece, Reece... She gazed at him in the swiftly enveloping dusk. At his dear, precious face, haunted by a hundred doubts and fears born of a desperately lonely childhood and miserable youth, an adulthood searching for something that had always eluded him until he turned his back on it and made a life on his own terms and conditions.

'And then I found out you'd been in love before...' he said in a strained, harsh voice as a muscle jerked in his jaw. 'I was crazy with jealousy that you'd loved someone—'

'For the whole of the time since we met,' she agreed softly, watching him with loving, passionate eyes as his head came up to search her face desperately, an incredulous hope beginning to burn in the silver depths of his eyes. 'Never before...' She stood up and reached up to him, winding her arms round his neck as his body froze at her touch. 'And I'll never love again if I can't have you. In that, if nothing else, I'm a true Vance—'

As his mouth came down on hers he crushed her into him in such an agony of love and relief that she could barely breathe, his need so great that it consumed them both as they swayed together in the soft, dusky air, touching and kissing and tasting.

'You'll marry me?' He moved his mouth from hers long enough to ask her and she nodded mistily, unaware of the tears streaming down her face. 'Oh, my love...' He enfolded her into his hardness with a husky groan. 'I could eat you alive.'

And then Wednesday set out to prove that he meant exactly what he said—much to Sunday's delight and undying satisfaction.

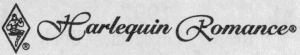

Harlequin Romance®

Coming Next Month
Four great books for Christmas—
all with a special mistletoe magic....

#3435 DEAREST MARY JANE Betty Neels
Mary Jane was a stay-at-home. She was hardly surprised when famous surgeon Sir Thomas Latimer seemed to have fallen in love with her glamorous model sister, Felicity. But Mary Jane didn't want Sir Thomas as a brother-in-law—she wanted him as a husband! Would her Christmas wish come true?

#3436 UNEXPECTED ENGAGEMENT Jessica Steele
Holding Out for a Hero
Love didn't play any part in Lysan Hadley's engagement. She liked her fiancé, Noel, and marriage seemed a sensible solution. Then Lysan was invited to spend the holidays with tycoon Dante Viveros. Lysan soon learned that there was more to life than being practical—and even more, she realized that she was marrying the wrong man!

#3437 A MISTLETOE MARRIAGE Jeanne Allan
Hitched!
Justin Valentine was a man who had everything...except a wife. She had run out on him two years ago. But now Cait was back, and determined to make this the best Christmas ever. She was no longer the spoilt little rich girl she'd been when they'd married, and she was going to prove that she would make the perfect rancher's wife!

#3438 ACCIDENTAL WIFE Day Leclaire
Fairytale Weddings—Book Two.
Harlequin Romance invites you to a wedding...
...And it could be your own!
On one very special night, single people from all over America come together in the hope of finding that special ingredient for a happy ever after—their soul mate. The inspiration behind The Cinderella Ball is imple—come single, leave wed. Which is exactly what happens to three unsuspecting couples in Day Leclaire's great new trilogy....

Nikki Ashton has to convince her boss, her sister and a whole assortment of relatives that she is happily married—ecstatic, in fact! Getting the wedding ring is easy, so now all she needs is for Santa to bring her a husband! Jonah Alexander seems perfect...if only he can handle ecstatic!

1997
Reader's Engagement Book
A calendar of important dates
and anniversaries for readers to use!

Informative and entertaining—with notable
dates and trivia highlighted throughout the year.

Handy, convenient, pocketbook size to help you
keep track of your own personal important dates.

Added bonus—contains $5.00 worth of coupons
for upcoming Harlequin and Silhouette books.
This calendar more than pays for itself!

 Available beginning in November at
your favorite retail outlet.

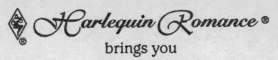
Harlequin Romance ®

brings you

How the West was Wooed!

We hope you've enjoyed our year of romance, Western style, so far! Now, with Christmas just around the corner, we have one more special cowboy for you—and he's about to be lassoed under the mistletoe!

Watch for:

#3437 A MISTLETOE MARRIAGE
by Jeanne Allan

Available in December wherever Harlequin books are sold.

And, if you like your heroes tough, rugged and one-hundred-percent cowboy, we'd love to hear your thoughts on our Hitched! miniseries. Do write with your comments to:

The Editors
Harlequin Romance
Harlequin Enterprises Limited
225 Duncan Mill Road
Don Mills
Ontario
Canada M3B 3K9

Merry Christmas, Baby!

A romantic collection filled with the magic
of Christmas and the joy of children.

SUSAN WIGGS, Karen Young and
Bobby Hutchinson bring you Christmas wishes,
weddings and romance, in a charming
trio of stories that will warm up your
holiday season.

MERRY CHRISTMAS, BABY! also contains
Harlequin's special gift to you—a set of
FREE GIFT TAGS included in every book.

Brighten up your holiday season with
MERRY CHRISTMAS, BABY!

Available in November at
your favorite retail store.

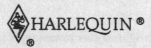